Falling For The Lawyer

Anna Clifton

EasyRead Large

Copyright Page from the Original Book

ESCAPE
publishing

ISBN: 9780857990334

Title: Falling for the Lawyer

Copyright © 2013 by Anna Clifton

www.escapepublishing.com.au

TABLE OF CONTENTS

Falling for the Lawyer

Anna Clifton

Alex Farrer has just one resolution: don't get sacked by the new boss that day. Enter one knight to rescue her from a run-in with a pile of mud. But will upending Alex's entire life be the next job on her knight's 'to-do' list, whether she likes it or not?

Legal eagle JP McKenzie has just one resolution: never get involved with a woman who won't stand up for herself. That is until a muddy Alex Farrer lands in his life with a crushingly big mountain of family expectation in tow. So what else is a modern-day knight to do?

About the Author

Anna Clifton is a lawyer by trade, a high school teacher in training and a mother to three children and a couple of cats. Her husband is not quite sure how her compulsive writing squeezes itself into the family schedule but like all good heroes he knows better than to stand in the way of the woman he loves on a mission.

Anna lives in Sydney but escapes with her family as often as possible to North Queensland where she loves to catch up on reading amongst the mozzies, crocs and cane toads—seriously! *Falling for the Lawyer* is her first novel.

Acknowledgements

My heartfelt thanks to Kate Cuthbert and the team at Escape Publishing for placing their faith in and deciding to publish *Falling for the Lawyer,* turning dream into reality.

To Romance Writers Australia and the dedicated staff who work there, thank you for keeping the dream alive at one in the morning when the writing efforts feel oh-so-futile.

Finally, thanks to my wonderfully wise and supportive husband and three children. Their zest for life is perpetually inspirational.

For John

Chapter One

'Whatever can go wrong, will go wrong.' That was Murphy's Law. And Alex Farrer knew with absolute certainty that her life had once again become the starring jewel in its crown of truth.

'Take charge of your life or it will take charge of you.' That was another saying to send a shudder through Alex. She only had to glimpse it running cheerily along the top of a desktop calendar page and it would set *her* running—in the opposite direction!

'Destiny is made in the decisions we make.' She was damn sure she was the pin-up girl for that one too—living proof that if you don't make a single decision for yourself destiny vanishes in a heartbeat.

Yet it wasn't for a lack of trying. Just that morning Alex had vowed to become the captain of her own ship of destiny. So what if her new boss's first job on his 'to-do list' was to sack her. She refused to take defeat lying down! She would seize the day, impress the socks off him and prove he couldn't possibly do without her! Finally, once and for all, she would take control of her own future! There was just one tiny little problem: life, as usual, had gotten in the way.

Alex stood on the kerb of the busy Sydney street, convinced destiny had just sniggered in her ear as a cocktail of mud and dirty water had risen like magic from underneath a passing truck's tyre and deposited itself all over her.

The pedestrian signal flashed green. Office workers huddling under umbrellas and lost in their own thoughts about the coming workday streamed out over the crossing. But not Alex. Alex didn't move. What was the point? Backwards or forwards the destiny trolls were lying in wait for her—either way she could kiss her job goodbye.

"Are you in some bother there, darlin'?"

Alex jumped. A man had emerged like an apparition out of the mist and rain at her side.

"I was waiting to get some money out of the cash teller," he went on, nearly shouting to be heard over the deafening torrents of rain tumbling around them. "I noticed you hadn't moved in awhile. Hey, you're right manky!" he declared suddenly as Alex turned to him and presented herself in all her muddy glory.

He began to laugh then—uproarious laughter drawing stares and smiles from passers-by as they took in Alex's appearance.

"Is it really necessary you draw everyone's attention to me?" Alex questioned tetchily while a remote part of her brain tried to work out what on earth the word 'manky' meant.

"I'm sorry." He suppressed his laughter but was unable to repress the Cheshire Cat grin. "But do you know that you are literally covered in muck? There's not a square inch of you that's clean! It really hasn't been your day, has it?"

"No, and it's about to get a whole lot worse," Alex thought out loud as she stared out through the rain, frozen within a miasma of panic and resignation.

"Well m'dear, you can't stand here all morning. What are you going to do?"

His accent suggested a childhood somewhere in the west of Scotland. It was lilting and musical, seeming to lean languorously into every vowel. And despite Alex's predicament it had a powerfully soothing effect upon her mood.

"I have absolutely no idea what I'm going to do," Alex confessed, her thoughts beginning to cascade back into her own problems again like the rain tumbling around them both. "If I go home to change and arrive late for work I'll lose my job, but if I arrive on time looking like this, I'll lose it anyway. Not exactly great options are they."

She could hear the bitter resignation in her own voice yet it wasn't really losing her job that was the problem. The problem was the train of events losing her job would trigger. If she thought her life was not in her own hands now she dreaded to think what it would be like once she was unemployed. In fact she'd been worrying herself sick about the prospect for weeks and yet fate had taken things into its own hands anyway, as it always did.

"Lose your job!" the stranger scoffed, still shouting to be heard over the dull roar of the storm which seemed to be hurtling towards them. "Don't be ridiculous. No one loses a job over a bit of mud."

"You do if your new boss is looking for any excuse to get rid of you."

The stranger studied Alex intently before taking her elbow firmly in his hand and guiding her away from the kerb and into the foyer of a nearby office block. There they found some respite from the tempest building around them.

"So this guy wants to get rid of you," he began again, resuming his posture of leaning enquiringly towards her as he spoke, his umbrella tossed to one side. "What have you done exactly, although you look like you could be trouble," he added with the flash of a quick smile.

"I'm not trouble!" Alex protested, choosing to ignore the teasing curl to his lips. "And as a matter of fact I haven't done anything yet, but he's arriving today and he's not called the 'Grim Reaper' for nothing."

"If you're not trouble then why are you at risk?"

"Because I'm an Assistant PA and my law firm has decided we're an unnecessary expense, like the biscuits in the tea room." Alex was staggered at the bitterness driving her indiscretion but at that moment felt completely powerless to rein it in.

The stranger's expression was thoughtful. "I see, and they call this new guy 'The Grim Reaper'," he repeated, his mouth forming an unreadable straight line.

"We're all dreading his arrival. No one in litigation thinks their job is safe with him around. Not that it's your problem of course," Alex added quickly, disconcerted by his increasingly pensive look as black clouds exploded into thunder claps above. "So thank you for your concern but I'd better go and find somewhere to get cleaned up."

"Don't be daft," he drawled, snapping out of his reverie at once. "You won't be able to clean yourself up under a tap in some ladies bathroom. Half that stuff on you is engine oil. Nothing less than soap, hot water and a change of clothes is going to sort you out but don't despair, I've got an idea. There's a frock shop up the road. I know the manager. She won't be open yet but she gets in early. We can get you a change of clothes in there and she'll have somewhere you can clean up."

"That's really not necessary," Alex objected; it was bad enough being in the hands of fate, let alone in the hands of a perfect stranger.

"I'm afraid it is necessary."

Again, Alex was distracted by his eyes as they rested intently upon her and waited for her answer. Nevertheless she tore her gaze away from his to look down at her filthy beige skirt, drenched cotton shirt and sodden black shoes. Biting her bottom lip she looked up at him.

"Is it really that bad?"

"Does The Creature from the Black Lagoon ring any bells?" He raised his eyebrows at her then in wry amusement.

Alex began to tug at the wet tendrils of her hair as she cast her eyes around her. She prayed some other solution might emerge out of the rain but of course none did. Once again her life was being tossed around by the forces of the cosmos as they played astrological tennis with her future—with grim resignation she admitted to herself that the man next to her was her only hope.

"You're sure this boutique manager won't mind?"

"Positive."

"And you're sure you have time to do this?"

"Aye," the stranger laughed at her. "And I'm sure there's not going to be an invasion of little green men in the next five minutes too."

"Okay then," she agreed finally, again deciding to ignore his sarcasm. "If you're sure it isn't too much trouble."

"I'm sure," he replied as the walk signal changed to green at the nearby crossing. "Come on."

Before Alex could object the stranger had grabbed her hand and was dragging her through unremitting sheets of driving rain, across the street and up the wide pedestrian mall on the other side. Alex ran as best she could behind him, her umbrella wobbling uselessly above her head as she struggled to keep up with his cracking pace. Finally he dragged her up the stone steps of a nineteenth century building fronted by a string of shops. It was towards one of these that he guided her when she stopped dead and shook her head.

"You've got to be kidding! I can't go in there!"

The stranger turned to her. "Why not?"

"You said a frock shop! That's not a frock shop. That's an exclusive boutique for customers with very exclusive black credit cards. Look, I really appreciate your offer of help but an outfit from there will set me back months."

"Don't worry, you won't have to pay for this. The owner's a pal of my ... of mine," he corrected himself quickly. "We can work something out with her."

Alex hesitated before replying, battling to get her head around why this man was going to a whole lot of trouble over a drowned rat he'd picked up on the edge of the street. "It's not that simple. You've been very kind but I'm afraid it's the end of the line on this rescue mission. There is no way a boutique like this will work something out for someone like me."

The stranger shook his head in exasperation. "God help your boss if you're this stubborn at work!" he declared before pressing on. "Now listen to me. This is how it's going to be. You're going to walk into that boutique and accept the help being offered because I *am* going to finish this rescue mission and I sure as hell haven't got all morning to spend on it."

He set his jaw then with a gritty determination Alex guessed would continue to rise with every protest she could throw at him. For some reason he'd decided to be her knight in shining armour and nothing was going to get in his way.

"All right then," she agreed finally. "I'll go in and see if there's anything I can afford but I know we're wasting our time. A single coat hanger from there will send me broke."

"Just don't make any decisions until you've cleaned yourself up and tried something on. Is it a deal?"

Alex nodded as she began to shiver violently in her wet clothes.

Together they approached the glass door of the boutique and left their sodden umbrellas to one side. A stylish young woman was moving about the shop and getting ready for the business day ahead. The stranger knocked on the door and caught her attention. She looked towards them in surprise but on seeing him at the door she smiled broadly and approached to unlock it.

"JP! Darling!" she cried, standing back to let the two of them in but barely acknowledging Alex's existence.

"Andrea, it's good to see you." He smiled, accepting her kiss on both cheeks.

"It's been too long! How's Caroline?"

"She's fine ... last time I saw her anyway."

"Oh ... I see!" Andrea nodded, her eyes roving over him with flirtatious interest.

Alex turned in surprise to the man she now knew as 'JP', intensely curious about the powerful sex appeal he had for this very stylish woman. But giving him the quick once over again Alex decided that despite the devastating effect he was having on Andrea, he was a very long way from drop dead gorgeous.

There was no doubt he was what a lot of girls her age described as 'built', but he wasn't especially tall. And he had a very ordinary, outdoorsy kind of face. In fact his knock-about looks suggested he'd spent far too many of his young years exposed to either the freezing cold of Scottish football fields or the blazing heat of Spanish beaches.

"So Caroline is still in the UK?" Andrea persisted, unfazed by JP's short responses.

"Yep, no plans to come here at this stage." JP gave Andrea an obscure smile. "Anyway, I didn't come in to discuss Caroline; I need to ask a favour."

"Of course, anything."

"This is...?"

"Alex," Alex interjected, remembering JP didn't know her name.

Andrea swung around to Alex for the first time and gave her a look as though she'd only just noticed she was standing there. Alex wasn't offended. She was used to being invisible to women like Andrea. But she was clearly becoming less invisible as Andrea's jaw dropped and her eyes widened as she took in Alex's hair, face and clothes.

"Oh dear! Do you know you are almost completely encased in mud? What on earth happened?"

"Alex had a run in with passing traffic and lost," JP offered by way of the briefest explanations. "She now has to front the new boss from hell and needs something presentable to wear so that she can get to work on time."

"I'll need to clean up first," Alex threw in, looking away from Andrea's stunned expression in appeal to JP.

"Would that be okay?" he asked Andrea.

"Of course. I've a shower and towels out the back."

Andrea moved towards a rack of clothing and removed some garments. "Here, this is a lovely outfit for the office. I'm assuming you *do* work in an office?" she added doubtfully, staring at Alex's dreary outfit before she draped a peppermint-coloured suit over her arm and began to lead her towards a door at the back of the shop.

Alex turned to follow Andrea but as she did a price tag on the outfit flipped over into full view. Four figures appeared after the dollar sign and behind Andrea's back Alex turned and shot a look of sheer alarm at JP, pointing to the price tag. He looked at it, nodded and then raised his eyebrows and pointed his finger at her as if to say, 'we had a deal, remember?' then that same finger rested against his lips to silence her protests.

"There's some shampoo in the shower recess," Andrea continued, unaware of the wordless exchange going on behind her before tossing at Alex with breathtaking directness, "Oh, and you'll find some heels out there as well. I'm afraid those shoes you're wearing just won't do at all—mud or no mud!"

JP McKenzie rose from the comfort of Andrea's lounge chair with jerky movements. He knew that if he didn't get up and walk about he'd soon slip into a deep, intoxicating sleep.

God he hated that flight from London. It absolutely killed him every time. He'd flown in three days ago and the jet lag was still eating away at his brain. And the problem was he needed his wits about him that morning, particularly as Alex Farrer had let it slip that every member of his new litigation section was dreading his arrival that day.

"Where on earth did you find that little poppet?" Andrea crooned from her large table, busy entering information into a laptop as they waited for Alex to return.

JP couldn't help but smile to himself. Andrea had only just met Alex yet she'd immediately relegated her to the level of 'poppet'.

How did women like Andrea know with such certainty who was in their social stratosphere and who wasn't? Caroline had been like that too; swift and brutal had been his ex-girlfriend's assessments of the women she associated with. You were either on her 'A-list' or you weren't, and once you were off the list there were no second round offers.

"I found her on the edge of George Street just after the mud thing." JP was wandering around the boutique, casting his eyes over the limited range of outfits on display. But he wasn't thinking about clothing right then, he was thanking his lucky stars fate had intervened on his side that morning.

But for the old man in front of him at the cash machine, struggling to master the challenges of modern banking, he would never have stood still long enough to notice Alex Farrer standing motionless at the pedestrian crossing.

She would have been so easy to miss too. Grey was the colour she'd conjured up in his mind: from a distance she'd been almost invisible against the backdrop of mist and city paving. If she hadn't turned at the very moment he was looking her way he would never have felt the lightning bolt of familiarity.

Once he'd captured a glimpse of her he'd been able to place her immediately. Quite a few times over the last couple of days he'd glanced at her photograph on the firm's website. And although he'd only had her profile before him as he'd waited for the cash machine he'd known instantly that the drowned rat standing at the lights was his new Assistant PA.

"You found her on the edge of the road and are now buying her a four figure outfit!" Andrea tinkled lightly. "I didn't know that inside that brash exterior was a knight in shining armour!"

"I have an ulterior motive," he explained in a low voice as he approached the table and rested his hands on it to lean closer to Andrea.

Andrea's eyes shone with conspiratorial pleasure. "And what would that be?"

"What that young lady doesn't know is she's my new PA and I'm her new boss and I've decided to have some fun in what is building up to be a day from hell."

"I see, but buying your PA a new outfit is an expensive way to have fun. Clearly you've got too much time on your hands, JP McKenzie," Andrea finished with a coquettish tilt to her head.

Andrea couldn't have been more wrong. JP had never been busier in his life. For months he'd been drowning in the logistics of merging his London law firm with the one partnered by his two best mates, Adam and Justin. Just to complicate things he'd also had to negotiate a torrid break-up of his two year relationship with Caroline, and that had drained him on every level possible.

"I can promise you I haven't had any time on my hands in ages." JP straightened again and shrugged his shoulders. "That means I haven't had time to spend any money let alone have any fun. It will be worth every dollar that outfit costs me when I see Alex's face in my office in about thirty minutes."

"I wish I could be a fly on the wall."

"I'll tell you about it some time."

"Well why don't we grab a meal ... some time," Andrea shot back in immediate rejoinder, raising her eyebrows in a way that suggested she'd be happy to be dessert.

JP swallowed in instinctive response. One of his ex-girlfriend's best pals was hitting on him and he hadn't even seen it coming—clearly he'd been out of the dating game too long.

His eyes flickered over Andrea. He took in the snappy short hairdo and the figure that was impossibly slender and curvy all at once. There was no doubt about it, she was a seriously sexy woman and he was seriously contemplating the not unattractive prospect of taking up her offer.

But as a critical bonus Andrea had those qualities in a woman that always attracted him like a moth to a flame: hard as nails, independent and ambitious to the core—just like Caroline. And just like Caroline, Andrea would never ask for anything from him beyond the shallowest commitment—no protecting, no encouraging, no emotional props would be needed—in short, the polar opposite of his mother.

JP opened his mouth to accept Andrea's offer but then quickly closed it again. Despite her perfection something he couldn't put his finger on was holding him back and until he knew what it was he didn't want to risk becoming tied up with another woman if his heart wasn't in it.

"Thanks for the offer but I'm not going to have time to tie my shoe laces over the next few weeks let alone go out for dinner."

Andrea shrugged easily and smiled. Thankfully she was unfazed by the knock-back. "So? Who's talking weeks? I'm not going anywhere over the next few months and my calendar is very flexible."

JP gave Andrea a bland smile in response to her suggestive one and was relieved to see out of the corner of his eye that Alex had reappeared in the shop. Nevertheless it took him a few moments to gather his thoughts and focus on Alex rather than the woman who'd just been offering herself up as a no-strings-attached date. Yet once the focus mechanism kicked in the rush of clarity took his breath away. For the second time in a minute he swallowed.

"Does it look that bad?" Alex blurted in horror as she read his shocked expression and began to fidget with the lapel of her new jacket.

JP gave out a snort of laughter. He rested back against the edge of the desk and folded his arms to continue his study of her. Andrea approached Alex with a satisfied smile and guided her latest model to an enormous mirror lining the wall to her left before leaving her there to answer a phone call.

Alex gasped visibly as she took in her reflection and JP guessed the sheer amazement of seeing herself in that extraordinarily beautiful suit was genuine. After all, the outfit she'd had on that morning was nothing short of a disaster on every level—even without the mud.

Alex's mouth remained open a little as she took in her tall figure; her legs looked like they went on forever in those silk pants. And JP couldn't help noticing the way the jacket tapered in at her tiny waist before blossoming open at the top of the silky black camisole she was wearing underneath. The whole outfit couldn't have fitted her better if it had been tailor made.

"Well, Alex, what do you think?" JP approached her from behind and studied the reflection of her heart shaped face and the silky dark hair with the fringe cut a little shorter than usual above her exotic eyes. "It will get you through today, yeah?" he added with a grin.

"It's the most sensational outfit I've ever worn," she breathed, clearly still shocked at her transformation. "But I'll feel totally like a fish out of water in this. Everyone will look at me." She was fidgeting again—this time with the jacket buttons.

"Of course they'll look at you—you look dead gorgeous. At least you will if you stop fidgeting."

"But I don't like people looking at me like *that.*"

"You mean you don't like *men* looking at you like that."

"It's not about the men. If I wear this then I'll feel like I'm ... I don't know ... trying to show off."

Only then did JP understand what the girl in front of him was saying. She was ill at ease with the idea that the world might stand up and take notice of her because she simply didn't want to be noticed.

Incredible!

For so long he'd surrounded himself with women like Caroline and Andrea who revelled in the world's spotlight, he'd completely forgotten there were women who hated it with an equal passion.

"Alex," he began eventually, trying not to sound patronising to this girl who fate had decided to throw in his path that morning. "You are what you are. Don't hide it under drab and shapeless clothing. You should dress up every single day and walk tall."

Alex gazed up at him, her dark chocolate eyes wide and thoughtful. She was processing his suggestion carefully before she shook her head in decided rejection of his proposition. "If I am what I am then why should I try and pretend I'm something I'm not?"

Suddenly the frivolity vanished from JP's mood. This girl was the real deal, the genuine article—no pretense or falsity whatsoever. And there *he* was pretending to be something he wasn't by keeping his identity from her. What had seemed like a bit of fun, as he'd described it to Andrea, was no longer feeling quite so funny. For with every passing moment Alex Farrer was becoming less like a ghostly grey apparition on the side of the road and more like a warm and charming girl. Worse still, she was obviously feeling fragile about the day ahead of her and her future was in his hands.

She'd been quite right when she'd said her boss would have to sack her in the next few weeks. The new policy at Griffen Murphy Lawyers was clear: no more than one PA to a lawyer. And as the latest equity partner to join the firm he would have to lead by example—Justin and Adam would make sure of it.

"You know we could stay here and have this conversation all day but I don't think it's going to get us anywhere." JP was now anxious to shut down the deception he'd begun as soon as possible.

"I don't mean to sound ungrateful about what you've done for me this morning," Alex explained as she swung around to face him. "You've been very kind."

"Do you like the outfit?"

"Of course I like it. How could I not? It's stunning."

"It's yours then. Keep the shoes too. Andrea said she could discount things; write them off as seconds, floor stock, whatever."

"I'll pay you back then," Alex announced as she swallowed and nodded her head in determined confirmation. "It may take me a little while but you'll get every cent. If you give me your address I can send you a cheque and..."

"My shout, Alex. I don't want you to pay me back." He knew her salary to the dollar and just how much it would hurt her bank account to do that.

She looked at him quizzically before whispering huskily, "You have no idea how grateful I am, JP, because you've no idea how important it is I don't lose this job..."

But Alex stopped then and snapped her mouth shut—too late. For after all his years as a trial lawyer JP was adept at hearing what people were not telling him, and right then all his instincts were telling him Alex Farrer was not terrified of just losing her job, she was terrified of losing her job at Griffen Murphy Lawyers in particular.

"What's so important about keeping your job at this law firm of yours?" He watched her expression carefully for any hint of what was going through her mind but the shutters began to close over her face.

"It's nothing, just family stuff," she said quickly, looking troubled and distant.

"We don't have time to go into it anyway," JP replied, silently resolving to get to the bottom of that comment some time soon. "It's eight-forty. Shouldn't you be at work?"

Alex looked at her wristwatch. "Oh hell! Yes! I have to go!"

"Then go," he replied with a short laugh of relief that he was finally bringing his charade to an end.

"Just like that?"

"Aye," he replied, surprised to hear himself lapse back into his Scottish vernacular. He didn't normally use that word outside of Scotland except when he was highly distracted—but Alex Farrer was nothing if not highly distracting in that suit.

"So after this amazing act of generosity I just thank you and walk out the door? It doesn't feel right. There must be something else I can do to show my gratitude."

JP's raw male instincts immediately launched themselves into man-land where all sorts of appealing notions of how he might like Alex to show him her gratitude threw themselves up at him, but he mentally shoved them to one side. He reminded himself about the difficult weeks coming Alex's way at his firm, but she'd apparently been able to read his mind because she was blushing furiously.

"Would you like to shake hands? Would that bring a nice, formal closure to this farewell of ours?" he finished with a teasing grin.

Alex nodded, clearly relieved at the formality which would end what in her mind would be their last minutes together, and it began as a handshake. The only problem was that a split second after that it was no longer a handshake. He was quite simply cradling her hand and pressing her long, cool fingers in his as she transfixed him with those eyes of hers that seemed to be busy scooping out his soul as though it was the bottom of an ice-cream dish.

JP couldn't have let her hand go if he'd wanted to and he didn't want to. Before he could stop himself he was watching her slightly parted lips and fighting off a powerful urge to find out what that mouth tasted like behind those lips. But with a quick summoning of willpower he got on top of the urge, released her hand and swung around to pick up her bag and pass it to her.

"Good luck today." He now really wanted her to go as soon as possible, disturbed at the direction his thoughts had been taking him.

Alex nodded and took a few steps backwards. He watched as she turned and waved goodbye to Andrea who was still deep in conversation on the phone but who managed a wave of acknowledgement. With a final glance backwards Alex Farrer flashed him a fleeting but serenely happy smile as she walked out of the boutique, leaving JP with a strong sense of foreboding that it might have been better for both of them if their paths had never crossed that morning.

Chapter Two

"Oh ... my ... God!" Sophie declared, deliberately pausing for emphasis between each word as she took in Alex's new outfit.

Sophie Reynolds, Acting Head of HR at Griffen Murphy Lawyers was resting her elbows on a workstation partition. She was deep in conversation with one of the senior PAs but her eye had been caught by her best friend wandering into the office as she'd never looked before.

Alex put her finger to her lips to hush Sophie before the entire office was alerted to the fact she was wearing a new outfit. Sophie nodded and winked at her conspiratorially, peeled herself off the partition and marched at breakneck speed around the office furniture to meet her friend at her desk. She grabbed Alex's hands and lifted her arms up to take in the full view of her new suit.

"Is that what I think it is?" Sophie demanded to know.

"Clothing?"

"Very funny, Alex. I know obscenely expensive designer clothing when I see it. Which bank did you rob to buy this?"

Alex laughed. "Nothing so drastic. It's just a second ... floor stock ... something like that," she repeated

JP's words of earlier that morning, awash with another wave of relief as she reminded herself he would never have an opportunity to make her feel *that way* again, for a woman should never feel *that way* about any man when she was engaged to marry another.

"Can I borrow it sometime, Al? No, on second thoughts don't lend it to me. It would be just my luck to spill tomato sauce all down the front."

"Soph, you can borrow it anytime you like. In fact you can have it. In the circumstances it might be better if you do. I'm not sure wearing an outfit bought for me by..." But then Alex bit down hard on her bottom lip. Sophie was her best friend but what possible good could come of her trying to explain the strange events of her morning. Unfortunately she'd stopped herself too late because Sophie's all-seeing green eyes were already searching her face like a roaming spotlight.

"Okay Alex, what's going on?" Sophie asked in her best interrogatory tone of voice as she perched on the edge of Alex's desk. "You're flustered and flushed and fidgeting with your hair in that way you do when you're really on edge. Something's happened to upset you this morning hasn't it?"

Alex bit her bottom lip as she lowered herself onto her chair, her handbag still hanging uselessly from her shoulder. She was wondering whether she could give Sophie a boring potted version of what had happened on her way to work that morning which would not bring on too many questions. But Alex wasn't sure how to condense her morning into that format. And Sophie's eyes were huge and expectant and Alex didn't have the heart to mislead her.

"So let me get this straight," Sophie began quizzically as Alex wrapped up the account of her morning. Her friend had been listening quietly with a knowing look but listening was at an end. "You get covered in mud. Some perfect stranger whisks you off to the most expensive designer boutique in the city, organises you into a new outfit and then says 'have a nice life'."

"Exactly!"

"No, no. You don't fool me. You're not telling me something."

"I promise I've told you everything."

"So he goes by the mysterious name of JP and you don't know where he works."

"No idea."

"And he doesn't know your second name or anything about you."

"He knows where I work but..."

"Ah huh!" Sophie declared victoriously and pointed a long, fire engine red fingernail at her friend. "He'll phone you."

"No Sophie, it wasn't like that. He has no intention of phoning me. And please don't suggest it anyway, it makes me feel more uncomfortable about all this than I already do."

"Alex Farrer," Sophie grabbed Alex's hand, resting it in her own and patting the top of it patronisingly, a wicked glint dancing in her eyes. Alex was desperately trying to think of something she could say to stop Sophie from blowing her meeting with JP out of all proportion, but her friend was already half way out of the barrier and was never one to be reined in once she'd made up her mind to sprint towards the finishing line.

"It's time we had another one of our little talks. You know, about life and the way it really is—not the way you think it is. Okay. Here I go," Sophie began in a singsong voice as though she was recounting a fairy story for a small child. "A red-blooded, I'm guessing quite attractive male, meets attractive young woman on side of road in distress. He rescues her from job loss by buying her four-figure outfit to wear to work. Then says 'have a nice life' and lets her walk away because he has done all of it out of the goodness of his heart."

Sophie finished her account breathlessly, raising her eyebrows at Alex expectantly as though waiting for an answer before shaking her head slowly. Alex couldn't help but laugh at her friend's exaggerated school prefect expression.

"Okay. Now I'll give you life as it really is. Attractive man meets wet and bedraggled but nevertheless alluring young woman on side of street in distress. Talks to her for a few minutes and then discovers he actually finds her *extremely* attractive and wants to get her into bed as soon as possible. Has more money than he knows what to do with so buys her an expensive outfit to woo her because he's already found out where she works and will be calling her later that day to ask her out on a 'pre-getting her into bed' date."

"Sophie, stop! It wasn't like that at all. Anyway, you're forgetting one show-stopping detail in this fairy story."

"Oh really? What's that?"

"Wet and bedraggled girl is engaged."

"Yes I know that but Sir Lancelot doesn't," Sophie retorted. "What's more, he has no idea he's just gone to all that trouble and expense over you for nothing. Poor guy!" Sophie declared, her eyes shining bright with incredulity. "I can't believe this has happened to you of all people. You're the last person who would go looking for it."

"Do you mean people go looking to be covered in mud on their way to work?" Alex replied, deliberately obtuse.

"You know what I mean. You're not exactly forward when it comes to winning attention from the opposite sex yet here you are, fresh out of the clutches of the original knight in shining armour."

"Have you ever thought that perhaps I'm not interested in that kind of attention from the opposite sex because I'm engaged?" Alex offered in ironic understatement.

Sophie scoffed and Alex immediately regretted raising that impediment; her engagement was one of Sophie's favourite hobbyhorses.

"Even if you weren't engaged to Simon you wouldn't look for attention from men. It's not your style. Anyway, you've been engaged to Simon for so long I bet you don't remember what attention from men feels like."

"Of course I do. Three years is not so long."

In fact three years felt like yesterday. One minute Simon was tinkling a spoon against a champagne glass to make a toast for her twenty-first birthday party and the next he was proposing in front of a gathering of more than a hundred family members and friends.

She'd been so stunned she'd simply nodded and smiled, desperately trying to conceal just how staggered she was that he'd ignored her point of view that they were too young to get married. But he had ignored it, adamant there was no need to wait. A long engagement would sort out any concerns she had, he'd said—and in a way he was right. She'd been surprised at how easily she'd slipped into her new status as an engaged woman, especially with family excitement and expectation wrapping around them both like a warm, comfortable cloak.

"How are the wedding plans going by the way?" Sophie's demeanour was mischievous. "Booked the church yet? The reception venue?"

"You know we haven't Sophie, but we're going to organise it soon."

"How about I take over the planning for you?"

Alex couldn't tell whether Sophie was winding her up or not. "No, that's very kind of you but..."

"I'm just kidding. No need to panic, Alex. I've no intention of bringing this wedding on before you're ready."

Sophie was right. Simon had been keen to get the wedding underway for quite some time by that point, and she had been dragging the chain on the wedding preparations. But it was so obvious to everyone that she and Simon were destined for one another there didn't seem any need to rush things.

She couldn't remember a time when Simon was not a part of her life. They were the original childhood sweethearts. Their families had been friends for years and they'd played together in the backyard as children. To say her parents adored him was the understatement of the century—Simon was the son they'd never had—and his family adored her too. They'd grown up in the same neighbourhood, gone to the same school and mixed within the same social network of families and friends all their lives. Their engagement had been a fitting together of two final pieces in a very large jigsaw puzzle that extended way beyond their two individual lives.

"What does Simon think about the upheaval within your office?" Sophie asked curiously.

"He doesn't know."

"You haven't told him?"

"Well nothing's happened yet ... and I don't think he'd care too much if I lost this job," Alex confessed as she swivelled absentmindedly from side to side on her chair, her heart sinking as she heard herself utter a near truth she found unsettling.

The actual truth was that Simon would be ecstatic if her ties at Griffen Murphy were severed. He wanted her to start concentrating on the wedding and their future home life. As he'd said last time they were together, she was in a go-nowhere job paying chicken feed. Why would she bother with a career at all when his business was going gangbusters?

There was just one problem—Alex loved her job.

"That's right," Sophie declared mercilessly as though she could read Alex's mind. "No need for the little wife to work when she's going to marry Mr Megabucks."

"It's not that. We want to start a family as soon as possible." Alex could hear Simon's so often repeated words echoing in her own voice. But Alex knew she was wasting her breath. Sophie had been raised amidst the expectation that career opportunities should know no limits. It was pointless to try and explain that the expectations swirling around her own life like mountain mist were so very different.

"Yes, well you are getting on," Sophie teased. "That biological clock is starting to tick pretty fast at twenty-four. Better get on with it."

"Stop it, Soph!"

"Stop what?"

"This ... this thing that you do about my engagement."

"Well someone has to try and gee you up! You're the most unenthusiastic bride-to-be I've ever met!"

"I'm not unenthusiastic," Alex argued as she felt self-conscious heat rise in her cheeks. "But when your fiancé lives overseas most of the time it's hard to plan a wedding. And work has been busy..."

"Okay. Okay. I'll stop." But Sophie wasn't half trying to conceal her look of concern as she regarded Alex. "Anyway, when do you think Jonathan McKenzie's going to arrive? You could cut the air with a knife in here this morning."

Alex looked around the litigation section of Griffen Murphy. There was a general buzz as people mooched around and chatted. No one could concentrate and few lawyers or PAs had started any work for the day.

Everyone in litigation had been on tenterhooks for weeks as news of the new partner had spread like wildfire through the office. Yet the day of his arrival was upon them. Just last Friday night they'd celebrated David Griffen's retirement as litigation partner and with a slightly sore head Alex had come in the day after to spring-clean the office in readiness for his replacement—Jonathan McKenzie, aka 'The Grim Reaper'.

"Who knows when he'll be here," Alex replied. "And we really shouldn't be so negative about him. He might not be the ogre everyone says he is."

"I'd love to share your optimism but where there's smoke there's fire. I told you my friend Megan has a cousin who worked for him when she was in London a few years ago. He won't hesitate to get rid of staff. If lawyers don't bill their hours they're gone. If they don't market the firm and bring work in they're gone. And as for PAs..."

"Yes I know. No more than one PA per lawyer and that includes partners," Alex recounted the gossip as it had been spread around litigation.

It made her sick with dread because Jonathan McKenzie's arrival simply had to be the sounding of the death knell for her position at Griffen Murphy. Then when her job was gone Simon and her parents would swoop. Not that he and her parents didn't want the best for her—they did. But they would look on a break in her employment as a great opportunity to navigate her towards marriage and family life. And without a rebellious bone in her body, Alex knew she would be the last person to rise up against a three year escalation of family hope and expectation. The fact that all she wanted was an opportunity to stop loving her job as much as she did before giving it up for her life with Simon was irrelevant.

"You never know, the new boss might make you the exception and keep you on," Sophie offered soothingly. But given that Sophie was Acting Head of HR, if she'd had any information to suggest Alex was not about to be sacked she would have thrown her that life line of hope already.

Alex shook her head in a gesture of rebuttal. "With Vera Boyd as senior PA to David Griffen these last twenty years do you really think the new partner's going to throw her over for some twenty-four year old junior PA? Face it Sophie, I'm toast."

"Don't be such a Gloom Hilda. No one knows for sure what his plans are. You're a smart cookie—you might land on your feet. And with any luck he'll soon see you can run rings around Vera."

Alex didn't share Sophie's confidence about that. For a start Vera Boyd treated Alex like the village idiot in front of the partners at every opportunity. More importantly, Vera was an experienced and impressive

PA. She'd been running David Griffen's practice forever. If Jonathan McKenzie sacked her five minutes after David Griffen's retirement there would be a stampede of clients from the firm. There was no way he would risk that.

Alex settled in at her desk and brought up the precedent files on her computer. She continued her ongoing work on the formatting but it was impossible to concentrate. Friends and colleagues were wandering past and wishing her luck for the day, yet their good wishes only served to make her more agitated.

Finally a ripple of excitement passed through the office. A rumour was circulating that the new partner was on his way down the corridor. The whole office became artificially quiet as everyone feigned industriousness.

"Good morning!" A male voice boomed across the office space. "Where are you all hiding?"

Alex's heart reared up in her chest and took off at a wild gallop, for that husky mellifluous voice was breathtakingly similar to the one still ringing in her ears from earlier that morning. But she immediately dismissed the notion that her knight to the rescue was now walking into her office in the form of her new boss. Fate had toyed with her enough that day when it decided to shower her in mud. There was no way it would throw her knight back at her in the safe confines of her own workplace!

Rising slowly to her feet Alex strained to catch a glimpse of the owner of the voice. Other members of staff were also rising from their chairs to approach and greet the new partner and a slight shift in the crowd finally offered Alex a clear view.

She'd doubted her ears but her eyes couldn't lie.

For there he was. Her knight in shining armour and the man she'd spilled her guts to about the Grim Reaper arriving at Griffen Murphy that day was at that moment wandering through the office and about to take up his position as senior litigation partner.

Alex sunk down into her chair and fought for breath as a cold sweat broke out all over her body.

He was moving along the corridors. Every now and then he stopped to be introduced to members of his staff but he was inexorably edging towards her like the tide washing in. And although she'd known that day would be difficult she'd never dreamed it would turn out to be the worst day of her life.

That voice again. It was asking every staff member in litigation to join him in the conference room. She'd had a reprieve for a few minutes and could breathe again, for now.

When most of the staff had filed in behind JP, Alex followed. She was reluctant to face him but there was no way she was going to miss what he would have to say to his new staff after the morning spent with his new PA and her bad case of verbal incontinence.

Alex sidled in behind the crowd of gathering staff. The conference room was packed with bodies and she was able to take up a position behind two of the tallest male lawyers in the section, declining their invitation to move in front so that she could see the man of the hour.

The atmosphere was electric as voices became hushed. Then that self-assured, sonorous voice with its dulcet Glaswegian tones cascaded into Alex's ears again.

"Good morning everyone," he began, "thanks for this impromptu meeting. I won't keep you long. I'd like to have a formal meeting with you all at a later stage to discuss planning for the office and I'll get around in the next couple of days to meet you all individually. I just want to say I understand this is a challenging day for all of you. I know many of you worked with David for a long time and it's difficult to change track. I ah..." JP paused momentarily, "I've been told many of you regard my arrival here as bringing gloom and doom. I must say I'm extremely sorry to hear that. That's why I've called this meeting—to try and set the record straight."

Alex tried to make herself tinier behind the bodies shielding her from the man she now knew was JP McKenzie. For she, Alex Farrer, Assistant PA and all-round office minnow, was undoubtedly the source of the senior litigation partner's information about his own self-confessed unpopularity. It had to be a bad dream yet unlike a bad dream she didn't seem to be waking up at the worst part. But perhaps the worst part was still to come!

"In fact..." JP began again, "I understand I'm affectionately known around here as 'The Grim Reaper'."

A guilty titter passed through the room. Meanwhile, Alex thought her head would implode with the pressure crushing her temples.

"Anyway, labels are neither here nor there. The fact is I'm here to do a job and do it well. I'm not going to mince words with you: this section is under-performing compared to other parts of the firm and litigation sections in other firms. I know we have a quality client base because I've looked at it. I'll also be bringing a very large client base to add to this. Having said that, I'm confident I've got good staff here and I intend to use what I've got. Rest assured though, there'll be changes made. Those who have capacity will have to take on additional tasks or leave. I'll be making these changes quickly as I've spent a lot of time looking at the staff and the work here. I already know most of you better than you think."

The hair at the back of Alex's neck stood on end as she wondered what he already knew about her, apart from the fact she was the most indiscreet employee of the firm.

At that point a young lawyer up the front of the room asked a question.

"I've been asked what the criteria will be for deciding who will lose their job," JP began again. "I should say I haven't made any decisions about anyone losing their job but I've found in firms of this size there are always a few who are determined to continue to do things their own way and not mine. Those people may as well start to look for alternative employment. What I'm looking for is dedication, loyalty and teamwork. I'm looking for people who believe in me and what I'm going to do here. If you're all those things you'll have nothing to fear but be warned, I can pick those who are not on my team at a thousand paces."

Alex was dizzy. Lowering herself into a nearby chair she wondered whether she should just shuffle out of her office and the building right then and there. What kind of future could she possibly have at Griffen Murphy? If her conversation with JP that morning was not evidence of a lack of dedication, loyalty and teamwork then nothing was. She probably wouldn't even last the day once he caught sight of her.

"Anyway," JP continued, "I hope you leave this room with the view that my arrival here is a great opportunity for the development of your professional careers. I'm sorry I've had to start my role here on this negative note but I was disturbed by the information I received this morning about your perceptions of me. I've been accused of many things in my time but I don't think anyone has ever accused me of being unfair. However I'm going to have to leave things there for now as I was due in a meeting five minutes ago."

JP was swallowed up by a crowd of people as he made his way out of the conference room.

Alex wished she could be swallowed up too, preferably never to be seen again. Her new boss had felt compelled to call a meeting with the whole of his litigation team and all because she'd blabbed her head off to a perfect stranger an hour ago. She'd undermined his first day and his expectations of their loyalty to him. He wasn't sure who he could trust and it was all because of her.

Alex sat motionless as her colleagues milled about her. They were chatting in hushed tones about JP's first meeting and the portent of his words. 'The jury's still out,' they murmured amongst themselves. 'No one can be sure whether jobs are at risk or not. He doesn't seem to be suggesting indiscriminate sackings of staff, only those not pulling their weight, or those who are not team players. That doesn't seem unfair but can he be relied upon to stick to it?'

As the conversations died away and people moved out of the room Alex rose reluctantly to her feet. She wandered out to her desk where she sat down heavily in her chair and threw her head down on her folded arms and groaned.

Was it actually possible her day could get any worse?

But then Alex sensed she wasn't alone in her workstation. A quiver rippled down her spine. She lifted her head a little to see a strong male hand resting on the desk next to her arm. She could feel breath in her hair and smell the fresh scent of male deodorant. It was disturbingly familiar.

Alex turned her head ever so slightly to try and confirm her fears were not being realised but before she could take her companion in with her eyes, her ears were already confirming the worst.

"Nice outfit, Alex Farrer."

Alex stopped breathing. By the time she'd started again JP McKenzie had vanished.

Chapter Three

"Come on, Alex," Sophie ordered. "Let's go and have a glass of wine. We've definitely earned it today."

Alex was typing furiously, so immersed in the task before her that she gaped at her friend for a few seconds before she was able to gather her thoughts and respond.

"Is it time to go?" Alex asked in disbelief.

"'Fraid so," Sophie nodded in mock irony. "I know it's a wrench to leave this place but you've simply got to go home sometime."

Alex was staggered. Somehow she'd managed to get through the day after all, and although the spectre of JP McKenzie's return had haunted her continuously she'd refused to stew on her predicament. Instead she'd put her head down and worked hard on David Griffen's remaining current matters. JP would need to turn his mind to them in the next twenty-four hours and with all the lawyers in the office so busy she'd decided to do as much of the legwork as possible to bring them up to date.

"I can't leave yet. I've got to get these memos finished."

But Alex was fibbing. The file she was working on could certainly wait until the next day. The real reason she wanted to stay behind was because she'd resolved to have things out with JP McKenzie.

No matter what lay in store for her she refused to wait for the guillotine to fall on her job at Griffen Murphy. She'd stand up to him and demand to know what his intentions for her were, even if that meant staying back for hours until he returned—if he returned at all.

"Have you anyone else you can go with, Soph?"

"Yes but I wanted you to come too," Sophie explained, pulling a face of exaggerated disappointment.

"How about some time later in the week instead?"

"Okay, but is that a promise?"

"It's a promise," Alex assured her and watched on distractedly as Sophie disappeared across the office.

She sighed then, apprehensive about how long she would have to wait for JP to return. Well, she didn't care. If she had to wait all night and catch him the second he walked through the door in the morning then that was what she would do.

She finished the work she was doing and then did some more filing as the office began to empty. By six o'clock every last person had left for the evening—even the lawyers. Alex was beginning to think she may very well have to wait until morning to see JP after all. But then the sound of loud, chirpy whistling greeted her ears. She froze where she stood at the filing cabinet, waiting to see whether her hunch that her new boss was heading back to his office was right. It was.

With his hands deep in his pockets and a distracted look on his face, JP McKenzie sauntered through the empty department he now headed up, a moving flash of dark blonde hair and dark suit. When he caught sight of her over the partitions his gait baulked a little before a smirk rose to his lips, his pace returned and he approached her.

Alex swallowed. All of a sudden her throat felt incredibly dry as she drove her gaze straight into those cobalt blue eyes that were already becoming familiar to her. "I was beginning to think you would never get back," she confessed out loud before she could stop herself.

"I have that effect upon people—tenterhooks, you know ... I'm kidding, Alex. If I'd known you were waiting I would have come down sooner. I was just upstairs talking to Justin Murphy."

"It doesn't matter," Alex replied dismissively, shaking her head a little to try and clear a way for her thoughts. The problem was that something strange seemed to happen to her brain when JP McKenzie was near, including blurting things to him she had no intention of blurting. "I didn't mind waiting. I'd like to talk to you."

JP looked hard at her and then cocked his head in the direction of his office. "Come on. Let's go in here. I'm glad you stayed. We've got a bit to go through."

Yes, like your job is at an end, Alex thought grimly as she wandered into his office, the panorama of the city skyline opening out beyond his enormous windows.

"It's been a long day and I'm definitely ready for a beer. Would you like a drink?"

Alex shook her head as he went to the small bar fridge inside one of his cupboards and helped himself to a light beer. He beckoned to her to sit down but she shook her head again.

"I'd rather stand," she said and remained where she was in the centre of the room.

He looked at her askance but didn't reply. Instead he moved to lean back against his desk as he lifted the beer to his lips.

"I need to know what's going on," Alex declared in an agitated rush. "I can't bear this uncertainty. If you're going to fire me then just do it now and let's have it over with!"

JP stared at Alex, choked on his mouthful of beer and carefully removed the bottle from his mouth. "You think I'm going to fire you? Now?" he spluttered.

"Why wouldn't you after this morning?"

"What exactly are you referring to? Have you passed a confidential document to an opponent? Have you stolen money from the firm?"

"No, of course not." Alex was flummoxed. It was not the reaction from him she'd been expecting.

"Then what?"

She searched JP's face for some indication of what he was thinking but his expression was unreadable. "This morning when I ... when I told you everyone here was calling you 'The Grim Reaper' and that no one wanted you to start."

His eyes crinkled at the edges. "Is that a sackable offence these days? I haven't done an update on employment law for a while. Perhaps it's time I did."

"But all your talk about loyalty, dedication and team players. I thought ... I was sure you were referring to me..."

JP threw back his head and laughed.

Again she was making him laugh. What was it about her he found so amusing? Sophie laughed at her too in the same way and most of the time Alex had no idea what she'd done or said that was so funny.

"Weren't you referring to me?" Alex was beginning to doubt lots of conclusions she'd reached about him that day.

He shook his head in disbelief before he spoke. "Alex, you don't strike me as the egotistical type to say the least. Nevertheless, you've got to understand you are not the centre of my universe in managing this litigation section. The fact is that I haven't made any final decisions about staff cut-backs yet."

"Oh, I thought..." But Alex couldn't utter another word.

"Is that why you've stayed back until now, because you thought I was going to fire you?"

She nodded and he gave her a smile that was so breathtakingly gentle she thought she would melt under its warmth.

"You must have had a God-awful time worrying about it all day, not to mention that disaster in the rain this morning."

Yet despite his gentleness Alex was beginning to panic. He was having that effect upon her once again—just like when he'd held her hand that morning, when she'd felt as though the whole world was compressing itself into one tiny space that only the two of them occupied—a space where there was no room for Simon, three years of family expectation or anything else. And once again she felt absolutely and thoroughly disgusted with herself.

"Come on, have a glass of wine. I think you might need it." Before she could object he'd returned to the fridge, pulled out a bottle and poured her a small glass. She accepted it from him before she could think of any way of politely refusing.

"I was positive you would sack me after this morning," Alex admitted, lowering herself unsteadily into one of the chairs near his desk. "Do you mind if I ask you something?"

He nodded, looking at her again in that deeply unsettling way of his, as if he'd never met anyone quite like her before—as though he was astounded to suddenly find her in his life.

"Why did you help me this morning but not tell me who you were? Did you know I was your PA?"

JP's eyebrows rose and fell guiltily. "Of course I knew. I'd seen your photo on the website but I wanted to keep my options open. If I was going to fire you I didn't want you thinking it was because you had some mud on your clothes."

Alex threw him a sceptical look. "Is that a sincere answer?"

"What do you think?"

"I can't tell with you."

"The truth is I felt sorry for you. I could see you were dead worried about today and I thought you'd be less likely to accept my help if you knew who I was. But I couldn't resist having some fun by surprising you at your workplace half an hour later. That was the unfair part of the idea. When I worked out just how unfair it was I wasn't prepared to rattle you in front of Andrea by revealing all in the boutique."

"It was all totally unfair," Alex objected yet she couldn't help smiling when she noticed the mischievous twinkle in his eyes.

He was an enigma, that was for sure. She suspected the most challenging part of her job would be learning to read his mind—if she had a job for much longer!

"The thing is," JP started again, more seriously, "I'm glad you told me how the staff was feeling. If you hadn't then the paranoia about me would have become worse over the coming weeks and then I'd have had no hope of anyone working with me to turn this section around."

"But I should never have said the things I said to you this morning."

"It was indiscreet, Alex," he reproached. "But in the circumstances of this morning I'll forgive you just this once if you forgive me for not telling you who I was. Do you think I had any impact this morning, with the staff I mean?"

Alex hesitated, stunned that he was asking for her point of view. "I think you've got them wondering."

"What does that mean?"

"Well before you arrived they would have preferred Jack the Ripper as new litigation partner. But since your talk this morning you've been raised up a notch to about Charles Manson level."

JP laughed. "Okay, quite some way to go then but what should I do to get them on side—you know them better than I do?"

Alex felt a warm tingling in her cheeks. Her new boss was asking her opinion about a management issue—she couldn't quite believe it.

"Why don't you organise something the whole litigation section can join in on—where everyone has to work together as a team—I don't know ... a footy match, something like that."

JP nodded thoughtfully, his mind clearly ticking over at her suggestion.

"How did you get such a bad name as a boss anyhow?" Alex asked as she felt the wine begin to ease the tension out of her taut and tired muscles.

"Maybe because I don't suffer fools," he declared suddenly, reverting back to command role. "But I suspect the truth is that someone who's fared badly with me in the past has spread some exaggerated rumours. Regardless though, I have a job to do here and I intend to do it. I'm not here to work on my popularity rating. By the way, where's my other PA?" He glanced towards the door as though Vera Boyd might suddenly materialise there.

"Vera's on two weeks leave. She gets back the day after tomorrow."

"I see. How do you two split the work up?"

'Vera splits things up and I get the dregs', was what Alex wanted to say. "Um, we just split it up between us, depending on how busy things are."

"Aye, right," JP replied and looked doubtful. All over again Alex felt her hopes sink as she remembered the firm's policy—no more than one PA per lawyer. Just because he wasn't going to fire her for spreading malicious gossip about him to perfect strangers in the street didn't mean her job was secure indefinitely.

"What do *you* do if Vera's covering the workload?"

"I work on precedents during the quiet times," Alex explained, hoping that wouldn't damage her prospects of holding onto her job. He could very well decide that a PA with enough time on her hands to create useless precedents was a PA he didn't need to waste a wage on.

"Precedents! What are you talking about?" JP asked with a sudden flare up of irritation. "I was told this section didn't have any precedents apart from out of date court documents."

"I started preparing them at the beginning of the year," Alex replied, convinced she'd just signed her own job's death warrant. "Vera was handling all of David's work on her own so I had time."

"Let me see them."

"What, now?"

"Aye, now."

Alex sat down in front of JP's computer and her fingers began to move across the keyboard as he stood behind her so that he could watch the screen.

"Here they are," she said finally. "We have a high turnover of junior lawyers who wander around the office looking for precedents they can use and I thought it would be helpful to put some standard documents together for them in plain English."

"I see," he murmured and leaned over her shoulder to read through the list. "Letter advising on mediation, containing Calderbank offer, proposing settlement conference, service of process, categories of documents for discovery, undertakings as to damages."

On and on he read, occasionally asking her to bring up a document so that he could skim its contents. He wanted to see everything, from documents in support of bankruptcy and winding-up proceedings to the various deeds of settlement and releases.

"Where did you get these from?"

"I kept an eye out for the good ones which came through David's office. Some came from the lawyers in this section. The rest I had to beg, borrow or steal from other sections."

"Has anyone approved these?"

"Not yet," Alex replied, remembering the various times she'd asked David Griffen to consider doing that, but it had never happened, probably because she'd always been verging on the invisible when it came to David

"All right then. I'll get a senior associate onto it tomorrow."

Alex twisted in her chair to look up at him. His features were rigid in concentration as he continued to scan the documents before him.

"You're kidding!" she challenged.

"No I'm not kidding. They're a valuable resource and as you say, a guide for the younger lawyers. At the end of the day everything has to be signed off by a partner but these will be a great time saver."

JP straightened then and moved across to the window. He was evidently deep in thought, his back to Alex as she shut down his computer. She drained the last of her wine from her glass and unsure what she was supposed to do next rose to her feet. She began to move towards the door but JP swung around.

"Where are you going?" he snapped.

"I thought that was it for tonight."

"But I need you to talk me through current matters."

"Now?"

"No, no, of course not. You go home," he shot back irritably with a wave of his hand towards the door. "There's probably a negligence claim on my desk that's about to explode but we won't let that stand in the way of clock-watching!"

"I don't call going home at seven-thirty clock-watching but perhaps they do things differently in the UK. Perhaps PAs don't go home at all!"

JP looked at her in bafflement as though trying to register where he was before dropping his eyes to his watch. "Of course, sorry. It's late. I must be operating on UK time. You go home, yeah?" he ordered with his usual ending for emphasis, changing tack to one that was conciliatory again.

"Aren't you going now too?" she asked more mildly, feeling guilty about ticking off her new boss when he was clearly as strung out as she was. "Despite what I just said I actually can stay if you need me."

"No need." Striding back to his desk he began to sort through files. "I'll check now for any bombs that might go off tomorrow."

"I can show you those straight away," Alex offered as she approached the desk and picked up a file. "By far the most urgent matter is this one. It's a passing-off and Trade Practices matter. The client phoned today. He's given instructions to brief counsel to commence injunction proceedings as David advised last week. I've prepared a brief..."

"*You've* prepared a brief?" JP gaped at her in open astonishment. "Why didn't you have one of the lawyers do it?"

"I asked but none of them could get to it before tomorrow. We've all been very busy in here over the last few weeks with David going. This is just a ... start...." She handed the brief to JP and he began leafing through it as she perched on the side of the desk.

"This is more than just a start—this is nearly there," he murmured when he'd spent the better part of five minutes reading through it. He raised his eyes from the file to meet hers with a penetrating look, his lips pursed and his eyebrows drawing together thoughtfully. "You've even prepared the Observations—my first impressions are they're first rate."

"They're just in draft..." she began but trailed off. Despite the fact he seemed happy with her work, perhaps she'd overstepped the mark. Perhaps she should have left the brief for the lawyers. But then another day would have passed before the brief was ready and the client's chances of winning the injunction could have been undermined by the delay.

"Okay what else?" he asked as he turned back to the files on his desk.

Alex gave him a potted version of each matter in descending order of priority until he held up his hand.

"All right. That's enough for me to be going on with tonight. I'll leave work on your desk for tomorrow. I'm stuck in a meeting all morning from eight so it will be good to know you're getting on with things."

He ran his hand back through the dark blonde cowlick of hair that fell forward across his forehead. He then sighed out loud and even though she'd only just met him Alex could read the acute tension about his eyes.

"I'm going to need a lot of support from you over the next few weeks, Alex," he began in serious appeal. "My partners are going to line me up in endless meetings and I'm worried about those matters of David's I haven't been able to get on top of yet. I'm deadly serious when I say I need you to be my eyes, my ears and my warning bell in this practice. The work you've done today tells me you can give me the support I need. Can I trust you to do this?"

Alex opened her mouth to reply but no sound came out so she closed it again.

"Why are you looking at me as though I've got two heads?" JP asked.

"It's just that I haven't had that level of responsibility in this job before and..."

"Why not?"

"David Griffen didn't..."

"Well I'm not David Griffen," JP tossed at her impatiently. "Based on what I've seen today I've decided you should have that level of responsibility and more. Are you up for it or not?"

"Of course but..."

"Good—then there's no need for buts." JP walked behind his desk, threw himself into his chair and dragged the top file in the pile towards him—he had hours of work ahead of him that night and as far as he was concerned their conversation was over.

It had been an abrupt ending to a gruelling day, yet Alex floated out of the building that night and she was in no doubt as to why. JP's belief in her was as pure as oxygen and sucking in great, greedy gulps of it she experienced a sense of soaring optimism as she never had before.

All of a sudden worries that had been eating away at her insides for months felt as though they were ebbing away. Suddenly, everything and anything seemed possible. Simon would understand that her dreams of a career at Griffen Murphy could fit into their plans for marriage and family. And Alex Farrer would have the guts to slowly but surely turn the tide of events that three years ago had begun to overwhelm her life. All she needed to do was believe in herself—as purely and simply as JP McKenzie did that night.

Chapter Four

"Alex, hold the door!"

Swinging around in the lift she'd just entered, Alex spotted Sophie weaving through the bustling morning crowd of office workers. She pressed the button to keep the door open and held it there until Sophie could burst inside breathlessly.

"Thanks Al, I'm late for a meeting so you're a life saver." She was panting breathlessly but was still able to take in Alex's outfit. "You've done it again!" she announced with a bright smile as the lift began to sweep the two girls up to the twenty-fourth floor.

"What do you mean?"

"Your outfit!"

"Oh, you mean this?" Alex looked down at the powder-blue suit she was wearing and ran her hand over the skirt self-consciously.

"Yes I mean that," Sophie mocked. "What else would I mean? Why are you suddenly strutting around like something out of Vogue?"

"I've had this hanging in the cupboard for months," Alex explained as they wandered out of the lift and into the firm's smartly decorated foyer. "I wore it to my cousin's wedding, remember? It seems a waste not to get some wear out of it."

But Alex knew she was dancing around the truth with Sophie. The truth was that JP's words from the day before had been singing in her ears as she'd stood in front of her wardrobe that morning. 'You should dress up every day and walk tall,' he'd told her. And so her hand had reached for the powder-blue suit. Other than the peppermint suit it was the only thing she owned which wasn't dowdy.

"It's not too dressed up?"

"No way!" Sophie protested vigorously. "I know you wore it to a wedding but it's really just a business suit—it's perfect for this place."

"Can I ask you something Sophie, as a friend?"

"Sure."

"You have to promise to tell me the truth, even if you think you'll hurt my feelings."

Sophie nodded in response. "What's up?"

"What do you think about the way I dress? I need to know."

"Ahh," Sophie responded portentously and bit down on her bottom lip.

"Please, Soph."

Sophie then pressed her lips together thoughtfully before replying. "Well, if you really want the truth, I think the outfits you wear are absolutely sensational ... for a fifty year old."

Alex winced yet felt no surprise. "I thought so."

"You're a gorgeous girl," Sophie hurried on. "There's no reason you can't change your style."

"I wouldn't know where to start. I'm hopeless. Even when you and I go shopping in the same boutique I come out looking like Laura Ingalls and you come out looking like Carrie Bradshaw. How on earth do you know what to buy?"

"Okay Laura Ingalls," Sophie declared. "When's your lunch hour?"

"Twelve-thirty."

"Meet me here at twelve-thirty then. You and I are going shopping."

"Are you sure you don't mind?"

"Are you kidding? I'll be Trinny *and* Susannah. I can't wait!"

But as Alex wandered through the office towards her desk just moments later she was wondering whether she should be concerned about the fact that the way she dressed suddenly mattered when it never had before? Yet in her heart she already knew the answer: it had something to do with the way JP had treated her the night before.

The bottom line was that she couldn't forget his reaction when she'd shown him the legal documents she'd prepared. And as she'd lain in bed that morning she'd begun to wonder whether there might be other things she could do that she'd never dreamed herself capable of. Self-belief was bubbling up within her and for some reason it felt important that she looked and dressed like someone who believed in herself too.

As she approached her workstation she expected to see a pile of files, left there by JP from the night before as he'd promised. Strangely though, her desk was bare.

She stopped dead, confused. She wandered into JP's empty office and checked his desk but no, nothing had been left there either.

Alex was puzzled. Had she misunderstood him about the work he would leave for her that morning? Weren't there several matters needing her urgent attention? It just didn't make sense.

"Looking for something?" A woman's voice literally boomed at her from behind, making her jump and swing around.

"Vera! You're back! We weren't expecting you until tomorrow."

"Evidently." Vera Boyd's cold, grey eyes were flashing and Alex was sure she could hear a snaky undercurrent to her tone.

Vera was a frightening woman. Alex had always been terrified of her—everyone was.

With David Griffen's approval, his Senior PA had ruled his litigation department at Griffen Murphy Lawyers for years. Alex had even heard of staff members mysteriously shifted out of litigation if Vera took a dislike to them.

"How was your break?" Alex asked, trying to invest their meeting with some normal social niceties.

Vera's grey haired bob bounced around her face as she replied, "The break was fine but perhaps I've been away too long."

"I don't know what you mean."

"Well it seems that in just one day you've managed to elevate yourself to Senior PA."

Blood turned to ice in Alex's veins as she absorbed Vera's barely contained resentment. Alex wished she could face Vera with nerves of steel but the older woman was just too intimidating.

"Don't pretend you don't know what I'm talking about," Vera snapped. "I saw the little love letters he left all over the files on your desk this morning. What kind of fool is he if he leaves that kind of responsibility to a sprat like you? He'll soon learn the way this place works. As for you, you've got tickets on yourself, haven't you? Who do you think you are, doing a lawyer's work?"

"There was no one available to do it yesterday ... it was all urgent."

"I'm no fool, Alex," Vera retorted. "We all know the rumour that the firm will only allow one PA per lawyer. If you think I'm going to sit back and let you flirt your way into Jonathan McKenzie's good books and freeze me out, you can think again."

Vera ran her eyes over her uncharacteristic but flattering outfit with obvious contempt and outrage rose within Alex as she'd never felt before. How dare Vera remove the work JP had left for her on her desk that morning? And how dare she hint that her dress choice and the work she'd done the day before had anything to do with freezing Vera out as a PA?

"I've never believed my job as Jonathan McKenzie's PA is secure," Alex grated out coldly. "But until I'm sacked or moved on I will do my job. That includes doing whatever he asks me to do."

"That's fine, Alex," Vera replied, spitting her name as though it sizzled on her tongue. "But you should be aware I'm on to you. I know you think you can bat those big brown eyes and wiggle that cute little backside and the boss will be like putty in your hands but he'll soon learn it takes more than a pretty face and a pert figure to run an office like this. He'll soon learn I've been around for a few years and know what I'm doing..."

"That's enough," Alex interrupted. "I'm not going to stand here while you insult me. I'd like those files back thanks—I've got work to do this morning."

"I've already taken care of them."

"What do you mean?"

"I don't know what Jonathan was thinking; a baby PA like you with work like that. It should be with lawyers. That's where it's gone."

"Do you mean you've handed on work to others that he asked me to do this morning?" Alex whispered in disbelief. "Who've you given the files to?"

"Yes, I've handed them on and no, I won't be telling you who has them."

"So what am I supposed to say to Jonathan when he asks me whether I've done the work?"

"You can tell him I've taken care of it, of course," Vera replied casually before turning on her heel and marching out of JP's office.

Alex could hardly breathe. For two years she'd had an impersonal but manageable working relationship with Vera Boyd—no more.

Somehow David Griffen's departure and Jonathan McKenzie's arrival had changed everything. As far as Vera was concerned the gloves were off. She was not going to risk losing her position as dominatrix of the litigation section over a little pip-squeak like Alex Farrer.

Alex wandered back to her desk, her hands shaking and her heart racing. Vera's vicious suggestions had left her breathless but was she right? Had she dressed up that day to impress JP and try to keep her job? Was everyone in litigation looking at her and thinking the same thing?

A warm rush of self-conscious embarrassment filled Alex's cheeks as she fought to overcome an almost overwhelming urge to run out of the building, into the first dress shop she could find and buy the saddest and most unflattering outfit available. Yet changing outfits part way through the day would only make everyone think she was crazy as well as ambitiously cunning.

Oh God, what a morning. To think she'd been looking forward to coming into work and all of a sudden her day was turning into a bigger nightmare than the one before. Perhaps Simon was right. Perhaps she was wasting her time trying to build her career in a legal office when marriage and motherhood were just around the corner anyway.

Alex slumped desolately into her chair. Having absolutely no work to do she spent some more time on the precedents but was completely unproductive. She was far too distracted by the nervous dread with which she waited for JP to arrive and find that not only was she idle but she hadn't done the things he'd asked her to do.

It was nearly lunchtime before Alex's phone rang for the first time that day. She'd guessed earlier that Vera had organised for JP's calls to be diverted to her own phone so when it finally rang it startled her out of her thoughts with a jump. Trying desperately to focus she swallowed and answered it with an efficient sounding 'hello'.

"Alex, it's me."

Alex's heart leapt. He didn't have to say who it was. She would have known that voice anywhere. "I've just stepped out of a meeting for a minute so I haven't got long. Has the brief gone out and the other work been done?"

Alex couldn't reply and silence reigned over the phone. How could she even begin to explain what had happened with Vera that morning and yet JP needed an answer and fast.

"Alex, are you there?"

"Yes, I'm here," she answered, the blood pounding in her ears.

"Can you answer me then? I don't have much time."

"I haven't done it," Alex blurted.

"You haven't done it!"

"No." Alex knew she should be trying to explain things but couldn't find the words to do it.

"I thought I could rely on you." JP's voice was rising in anger and disbelief on the other end of the line.

"You can, JP..."

But he was too furious to wait for the end of her sentences. "Clearly I can't. I had a good feeling about you Alex, about how we could work together, but I must be losing my instincts."

"JP please, let me explain..." Alex begged, but he was too riled with her.

"I haven't got time to hear your excuses. Anyway, what possible excuse could you have to let me down on this when the notes I left on your desk made it clear you were to deal with these matters first thing this morning. Have you got the files with you?"

"No."

"Then who does?"

"Vera knows where..."

"Vera? Is she back? Thank goodness. Put me on to her straight away."

"JP..." Alex began again.

"Now!" he demanded down the phone.

Alex had no choice. With the touch of a couple of buttons she directed his call to Vera's extension and then dropped her head into her hands and moaned.

She could just imagine the conversation JP was having with his Senior PA right then. Vera would be putting a favourable spin on things so that she came out of the incident looking like the PA of the century and

Alex like a walking disaster area—her fate as an unemployed Assistant PA had to be sealed!

"Alex, what are you doing lolling all over the desk when you were supposed to meet me at the lift ten minutes ago?" Sophie was at her side and looking down at her, her hands resting on her hips in irritation.

"Soph, I'm so sorry! I completely forgot about the shopping arrangement."

"Did you skip your swim this morning? You know how flaky you get when you do."

"No, I didn't miss my swim. And I'm fine Sophie, I've just had a run in with Vera and Jonathan, that's all. Do you mind if we take a rain check on our shopping?"

"Yes, I do mind," Sophie replied without hesitation. "If you've had a run in with Vera and the boss then the last thing you should do is mope around here all lunch time. Come on. Let's go."

"But I'm not in the right frame of mind for choosing clothing."

"Don't worry about that. I am. I'll choose everything for you. All you have to do is dress up."

Sophie grabbed Alex's bag off the back of her chair and strung it over her friend's shoulder. And it wasn't long before Alex was admitting to herself that she did feel a lot better for escaping the office for a while.

She spent an hour trying on outfits as Sophie draped her in clothing and accessories. Before long she had a pile of gear on the shop counter and her credit card was running through the machine.

"I just hope I have a job next week to pay for it all," Alex said to Sophie as the two of them wandered back into the foyer of the building amongst the lunchtime throng. But when Alex saw JP emerge from the lift and unknowingly begin to walk straight towards her she stopped dead in her tracks.

Her next set of instincts told her to turn and run but she was unable to move. A confusing cocktail of anxiety about the outcome of that morning, irritation with him for not allowing her to explain herself and a deeply disturbing desire to be in his company again was coursing its way through to every nerve ending in her body.

Unaware her friend had stopped behind her, Sophie had continued on into the lift, chatting cheerily to the now empty space beside her. Behind her in the crowd, Alex remained rooted to the ground.

JP's eyes swept over her and then back again, his lips pressing together as his gaze drifted over her figure in the powder-blue suit. And as he approached she waited for the rebuke, yet JP didn't seem to have any particular interest in launching into a tirade of chastisement. He stood close to her as the crowd jostled them a little, his hands deep in his pockets in his characteristic stance.

Alex lifted her chin to face him. There was no way she would apologise. She'd done nothing wrong. If he wasn't prepared to listen to her side of the story then that was just too bad.

"Well?" he began finally when she maintained her stony silence.

"Well what?" she grated.

"You owe me an explanation."

"It's a bit late now. I'm sure you've already had Vera's take on what happened."

JP smirked humourlessly as he absorbed the hostility in Alex's voice. "As a matter of fact, I have. Now I'd like your take."

"What would be the point? I'm just Vera's assistant. Why would you take my word over hers? I suppose she's blamed me for everything that happened this morning."

"She has."

Fury and indignation coursed through Alex like floodwaters. "How dare she! Short of going around to every lawyer in the office to beg for the files back there was nothing I could do to get your work done. I wasn't about to humiliate myself like that just because Vera pulled rank and took them all away from me."

"Is that right?"

"Yes, it is."

"So why are you so angry with me?" he queried, raising his eyebrows.

"Because you didn't give me a chance to explain."

"Perhaps you should look at this from my point of view. I leave an important meeting to find out whether or not my PA's done the things I asked her to do, only to hear her blabbering unintelligible monosyllables."

"I was getting to the point when you cut me off!"

"I didn't have time to wait for you to get to the point!" he dismissed her hotly.

"Then perhaps you shouldn't jump to conclusions!"

At that point JP rolled his eyes to the heavens and dragged a hand through his hair in exasperation. He appeared to be trying to compose himself before he lowered his gaze to her again and began to speak. "Alex, do you have any idea how much I've got on my plate?"

She nodded. "Of course."

"Can you understand how I feel when I find myself dragged out of a meeting to deal with a demarcation dispute between my two PAs? Can you understand I might have trouble finding the patience to allow you ten minutes to give me your side of the story?"

Alex stared at him. Although she still felt annoyed she couldn't dismiss his point of view. She opened her mouth to make this concession when she was suddenly given an unintentional shove from someone in the crowd behind her and was hurled straight into JP's arms.

Instinctively she threw her own arms around his neck for support but he was already bearing her weight. His hands were at her waist, warm and strong underneath her suit jacket. She lifted her face to his and was bathed in a white heat radiating from his cobalt blue eyes. They were gleaming very brightly with a need she'd never seen in a man before, a predatory gleam that was at once exciting and terrifying.

He could have let her go then. She was steady enough to stand on her own two feet. But he didn't. For three long seconds that felt like hours he held her against him, his body heat mingling with her own, the subtle aromas of his musky aftershave filling her senses.

How Alex wished she could explain it away. How she wished she could dismiss it as a meaningless hesitation to act on his part. But JP's eyes were locked with hers the whole time, confirming the treacherous swing bridge of possibilities that had been thrown up over the canyon dividing them—a canyon more vast than he could ever begin to imagine.

"Are you hurt?" he whispered huskily, urgently.

"No, I'm okay, thank you," she murmured back and then with a sickening lurch of her stomach she remembered who she was and the promises she'd made to another—Simon.

Somewhere in New Zealand Simon was working hard for their future, unaware that his fiancée was lolling about in the arms of her new boss, her body moving into nothing short of primeval overdrive at his touch.

A deep, all pervading rush of shame swept through her as she extracted herself from JP's supporting hands to put distance between them.

"I'm sorry," she muttered quietly.

JP watched her intently, his expression taut with self-restraint. "Don't be. You liked that as much as I did."

"I didn't."

"Well if that's what it's like to hold you when you don't want me, I'd love to have you in my arms when you do."

"Don't JP ... please. You're my boss," Alex implored, mortified by the all-consuming physical urges that still held her in their grip.

She was at a loss as to how to ward off the effect he was having upon her, ignorant until that moment that men and women could feel for each other what she was feeling for JP. She'd always been sceptical of those chick flicks where couples were almost out of their minds with desire for one another. She'd always assumed they were so far removed from reality it was almost laughable. Yet there she was, in touching distance of a man who she could hardly think straight around, who seemed to reach for a woman inside her no one had ever known before—a woman she hadn't even dreamed existed until that moment.

"You're right," he said after a seemingly interminable silence. "Those comments were unforgivable. I apologise."

"Let's just forget it happened," Alex suggested quickly.

JP nodded in response and his eyebrows drew together. "We need to talk about how we're going to manage the work allocation from now on." He straightened and shrugged his shoulders as though that would put the required formality back into their exchange. "I can't have a situation arise again where I don't know what's going on in my own office but I think I have a solution."

"What is it?"

"Not here," he replied, shaking his head. "I'm out now for a few hours but I want to talk to you when I get back. Will you wait?" He was pinning her down with his eyes and she couldn't refuse him anything when he looked at her like that.

"I'll wait ... but this afternoon..."

"I've been in the office for the last hour so there's more work on your desk," he replied immediately, reading her thoughts. "If by any chance it's been removed again I want you to call me—but I don't think that will be necessary."

And right then Alex knew she wouldn't have to explain the trouble with Vera that morning. Somehow, JP understood what had happened between his two PAs. He knew she was blameless in the whole affair, despite any account Vera may have given him to the contrary.

JP continued through the foyer then and out of the building into the bright afternoon light as a strange possessive longing for something she needed or wanted surged up in Alex's chest.

Simon. That was what she needed.

He'd been away too long and she was missing him. That was why her head was scrambled. If she could just see him again she knew her confused feelings for JP would disappear. But seeing Simon was impossible and so she reached for the next best thing.

Alex hit the fast dial button on her mobile phone. After a few rings a familiar voice greeted her from the other end.

"Hi Hun," Simon's up-beat voice reached her from thousands of miles away.

"I just wanted to ring, to hear your voice and make sure everything's okay."

"Everything's fine, Al. Why do you ask?"

"No reason. We just haven't spoken for a few days, that's all."

"I know. I know. I was going to call you last night but got caught up in a meeting."

"That's okay. I know you're really busy."

"How's everything with you? Has the Grim Reaper arrived?"

"Yes," Alex said, but hoped the conversation wouldn't centre on the very man she was desperately trying to put out of her mind.

"How's he going? As bad as everyone expected?"

"No, not exactly," Alex replied, flailing around for neutral responses as she ran a trembling hand through her hair.

"Well, if I have my way you won't have to suffer him for too much longer."

Alex tensed, knowing Simon was leading up to an announcement of some kind. "What do you mean?"

"Just business. Nothing you need to trouble your pretty little head about."

Alex hated herself for the irritation that prickled her skin. She was sure Simon didn't mean to be patronising when he dismissed her like that. Normally it didn't bother her too much that he wouldn't discuss business with her—and he never did—but it rankled her today.

"You know how I hate surprises, Simon," Alex replied with a strong hint in her voice that she wanted to be told what was going on.

"You'll know soon enough," he resisted, oblivious to her meaning.

Alex gave up. He'd stopped listening to her on that subject and she knew it would be useless to press. "Are you looking after yourself?" she asked, preferring to change the subject.

"Pretty much, probably a bit too much fast food. But when you're in and out of meetings you can't always sit down to a proper meal. Let's just say I'm looking forward to some of your great home-style cooking—almost as good as my mum's you know. Oh, that reminds me, guess who was in Auckland and rang me."

"Who?"

"Your cousin, Monique. She's been travelling around the North Island."

"Really, I didn't know she was over there," Alex replied, glancing at her watch to see that the afternoon was heading for two o'clock.

"Nor did I. Anyway, it was great to see her. She was staying in an apartment and cooked a meal for me."

"That was nice of her."

"Wasn't it," he agreed chirpily.

"Simon, I'm sorry this is a short call. I just wanted to say 'hi' but I'd better go now, I'm late back from lunch.'

"Okay, no problem. I'll be talking to you sooner than you think anyway."

Alex paused on the other end of the line. "Will you? How come?" she queried again at his thinly veiled reference to a change of plans but it was too late. Either the call had dropped out or he'd rung off thinking their conversation was at an end.

Despite the mystery boxes he'd thrown at her Alex was glad she'd called. It was reassuring to hear his steady, self-assured voice on the other end.

She felt back on track again and that was how she was supposed to feel: calm and together and not as though she was on an emotional precipice. Why on earth would she be feeling on a precipice anyway when she had everything a girl could want or need: a devoted fiancé, a loving family and a job she enjoyed, at least in the short term. And with that thought lingering as she headed back to work, Alex felt ashamed of having wondered whether what she had might never feel like enough again.

Chapter Five

Alex had a lovely afternoon.

Vera stayed out of her way and she had plenty to be going on with. JP had left a stack of files on her desk adorned with countless yellow post-it notes containing cryptic instructions in his scrawling handwriting.

One thing that did strike Alex as a little strange was that the work he'd left for her involved more drafting and research than she'd ever done before. It was not really work which a PA would ordinarily do. She could only guess that Vera had been left to type JP's letters, manage his diary and take his telephone calls but Alex wasn't about to go in search of her to find out.

The afternoon disappeared in a flash. Before long, other PAs were turning off computers and organising their desks for the following day. There was still no sign of JP but Alex didn't mind. It gave her more time to steel herself for their next meeting. And she'd resolved that once that was over she would find a way to do her job and keep her distance from him at the same time. Some brief exchanges at her desk or in his office were all that were necessary. If she could stick to that then their conversations could be kept short and business like.

With those thoughts churning in her mind she worked into the early evening. By that time she was confident she'd scaled and conquered her fears about the effect he was having upon her, so it was with dismay that she found her pulse leapt out of the barrier as soon as she heard his voice across the office.

He was talking to two lawyers about their working arrangements and current matters. Alex tried to focus on her work but it was useless; she couldn't help but follow every part of his conversation.

He seemed to be able to walk the treacherous line between authority and equality. She could tell the lawyers were hanging on his every word yet they shared jokes and he listened to their suggestions. If he didn't agree with them he had a way of putting his views back to them without criticism. Alex was transfixed.

Finally their conversation wound up. She could sense he was moving towards her and got to her feet to meet him in an effort to keep things formal.

"Would we be able to have that conversation about work allocation now?" she asked as he approached.

"No problem."

Alex nodded and followed him into his office. He closed the door behind them.

"Take a seat." He moved to sit behind his desk, locking his hands behind his head and leaning back in his chair. "I want you to change jobs," he announced in a business-like fashion before she could say anything.

Alex knew her expression was dissolving into a running palette of shock and dismay. Studying the change in her in curious fascination, JP withdrew his hands slowly from behind his head and leaned forward, resting his elbows on the desk.

"Alex."

"What?"

"I don't mean leave the firm ... or my office. I'm not sacking you."

Her baffled dark-eyed gaze met his across the desk. "You're not?"

"No. I want you to change roles," he explained, smiling at the way she always assumed the worst possible outcome, waiting for the axe to fall on her life. "I don't want you to work with me as a PA any longer."

Alex was still looking at him in bewilderment.

"I'm going to offer you a role as a paralegal so that you can start studying law. I've looked up your leaving results and quite frankly, with those marks it's a crime you're not already through a law degree and working as one of my solicitors. Anyway, we can't turn back time but we can sort things out now. You'll have no trouble getting into one of the part-time courses so that you can keep working here."

Alex gaped at him. She seemed incapable of speech.

"You must have considered this," he prompted, wondering whether she would ever contribute to the discussion.

Alex shook her head in dumb response.

"You haven't?"

"Not in such detail ... the move to a paralegal position ... none of that."

"How can that be possible? You have raw instincts for the law and there's no doubt you have the academic ability. Most importantly though the work you've done here tells me you're just downright passionate about it. You couldn't have applied yourself and acquired the knowledge you have without having done extensive reading. Is that right, Alex? Have you been teaching yourself law in your own time?"

"Not teaching myself exactly, but I read our Counsels' advices, and I read books from the library here so that I understand the work I'm doing. But I've been happy working as a PA. I can't become a lawyer JP, not now."

JP rose to his feet and wandered over to the window, keeping his back to her. He needed to have her out of his line of vision to collect his thoughts for a minute.

The conversation was not turning out the way he'd expected because he'd expected her to leap at the fabulous opportunity he was offering her. In fact, who was he kidding? He'd been looking forward to telling her—looking forward to making her happy.

"I had no idea you'd resist this," he began again in disbelief as he swung around to her. "You don't seem to understand. I've spoken to my partners about it. Every year the firm offers one paralegal a generous grant towards university costs. You'd have to write a four thousand word essay on ethics but that won't be a problem for you. You'll blitz it, Alex."

"Thank you, but I can't accept," Alex replied, a flat but determined edge to her voice.

Sensing she was in the process of erecting a brick wall between them JP dragged a chair near her and sat down.

"Okay Alex. I'm being frozen out here but I need to know what's going on in that head of yours." He was straining to keep his voice from rising in frustration.

"You've made me an offer and I've declined," she shrugged. "So I guess that means my position as an Assistant PA has disappeared."

"This has got nothing to do with getting rid of your position," JP replied angrily. She was definitely shutting him out and he had to stop that happening before she slipped out of his reach altogether.

"Even if the offer hasn't got anything to do with the PA position," she went on in a businesslike monotone.

"I know you're policy on PAs so we may as well sort that problem out right now. Today's demonstrated there's no shared role here for Vera and me."

"You're right about that. I don't need two PAs but I *do* need a paralegal and you're the best candidate."

"I'm sure there are other PAs who'd jump at the chance."

"I don't want anyone else!" JP almost shouted. He rose to his feet again and began to pace the room, shocked at the passion behind his last outburst. "Why don't you want to become a lawyer?" he asked, trying to steady his voice and break down her obduracy with a technique he was comfortable with: cross-examination.

"That's a silly question. Why don't you want to become a hairdresser ... or a vet ... or a mechanic?"

But JP heard the tiniest of wobbles in her voice. He had to keep prising her open before she clammed up again.

"Don't be obtuse, Alex," he replied slightly more calmly than before as he threw himself onto a chair near hers. "Is it the study you're worried about?"

Alex shook her head.

"Is it the balance of the fees you'll have to pay? You'll be on an increased salary as a paralegal you know. It will cover things. And it doesn't mean you're bound to the firm—there's no pay back if you decide to leave."

"No, it's not any of those things!" Alex almost cried out and he knew he'd nearly cracked her open, the strain visible around her eyes.

"Is it the long hours, or the difficulty of the work? I can help you with that..."

"I'm engaged!"

Silence descended upon them both like a blanket.

During his years at university a lecturer had once passed on to JP the age-old legal adage: never ask a question in cross-examination when you don't have a damn good idea of what the answer will be. He knew he'd just fallen seriously foul of that rule for the first time in his career. "You're what?"

"I'm engaged to be married."

Without thinking about the utter inappropriateness of what he was doing JP reached for her left hand and took it in his. Caressing her long fingers he stared in particular at the one where the engagement ring should have been.

He knew he had no right to touch her or speak to her like that but in the short time he'd known her she'd gotten right under his skin. Her commitment to another man wasn't resonating with the instant rapport, the chemistry, the frisson, whatever you wanted to call it, that had wrapped the two of them up in knots from the moment they'd met.

"Why aren't you wearing an engagement ring?" Without looking up he let go of her hand. "They do serve a number of purposes you know, one of which is to stop men making complete fools of themselves around engaged women."

"We haven't gotten around to buying one because my fiance's been living in New Zealand but he's coming back here to live—very soon."

"How long have you been engaged?"

"Three years."

"Three years! Why on Earth would anyone become engaged for three years? Who is he?"

"His name's Simon."

"Simon. For three years. And you've never gotten around to getting an engagement ring, let alone getting married. What does he do, this Simon?"

JP watched on as Alex drew herself up in defensive response. "He manufactures clothing. And it's not like that ... the way you're putting it ... you're twisting it around ... making it sound like I don't want to get married."

"Do you want to get married?"

"Of course."

JP paused before throwing caution to the wind. He needed to see her reaction to the next comment. "Forgive me if I say the signals you've put out to me are not consistent with a woman who's head over heels in love with another man."

"Don't you think I know that?" Alex threw at him wretchedly and tore both her hands through her hair. JP watched on as a look of sheer agony and despair moved across her face. "I don't know what's wrong with me and I feel sick about it!"

JP wondered whether he'd been with Caroline so long he'd lost his ability to read women but Alex's reaction told him all he needed to know. She had feelings for him, just as he had for her, but unlike him she was worried about those feelings—very worried.

"When I pressed you about doing law you told me you're engaged. They don't bar married women from the law you know so are those two things connected?"

"No ... yes ... I don't know," Alex's words scattered in the air around them like pinballs.

"Tell me what's going on, Alex." JP heard the imploring note in his own voice but was powerless to stop it. "I need to know what your future is."

"Simon and I are getting married," she explained, her eyes wide and dewy. "The plan has always been that when that happens we'll have children and I'll give up work. I would disappoint every single person I care about if I turned around now and locked myself into a law degree and a demanding career for years on end."

"Who the hell are these people who want to keep you from doing the thing you love!" JP barked. Her explanation had hit a nerve. "It's your life. It's your decision. You're not married yet."

"But it's not just about me. In my family, we don't make decisions in isolation from everyone else because they don't affect just one person. Everyone's happiness is interwoven with everyone else's. You probably think that's silly and old-fashioned but it takes much more than one or two generations to forget centuries of tradition."

"I know about tradition!" JP nearly spluttered as memories of his beloved mother, crushed by the regret of her own shattered dreams swamped him, making it hard to breathe. He was damned if he was going to sit back and watch Alex give up on her future before she'd even started it, just as his mother had. "And traditions have a place. But Alex, the one thing that's universal is love and I'm sure your family loves you. So tell them what you want to do with your life. They'll understand."

"It's not that easy," Alex sighed. He could tell she was already emotionally wrung-out by the conversation and wondered how it was possible to be so young and yet already carry a lifetime of regret.

"Have you ever thought about enrolling in law, Alex? And I want the truth."

Alex looked long and hard at him before nodding. "I took legal studies at school and was social justice captain too—I would have liked to work with people in need, but it's not to be," she added in a hoarse whisper.

"You'd like to become a lawyer then?"

"Yes, but it's a pipedream, JP. It's not going to fit into my life."

"Rubbish!" he handed down his verdict without mercy. "If you want something badly enough you can make it fit in. If your family loves you they'll see it's what you want and they'll support you."

JP sat back in his chair with a thud and rubbed his whiskery chin thoughtfully before throwing himself forward again. His mind was racing as he formulated a plan.

There was no point forcing her into a decision that night—she was too shattered to decide anything. But he could stall her from deciding against it completely and that would give him time to work on her.

"Will you promise me something then—just one thing?" he asked eventually.

"What?" Alex replied, her voice empty and miserable.

"Will you promise me you'll think about my offer for at least one week before you give me a final answer?"

"It won't make any difference. You know what a legal career does to a woman's life and that's not the life I committed myself to three years ago."

"Just promise me, that's all I ask, yeah?"

"Okay. But what if I decide 'no'? I guess that means I'm out of a job."

"I haven't worked that out yet," he answered, remembering Adam and Justin were expecting him to resolve his PA issues sooner rather than later. "I was so sure you'd agree to the paralegal offer. It seemed like the perfect solution. I thought it would be what you want and it would be what I need..." But JP caught himself up mentally and didn't go any further.

"I think I must have misled you about my intentions.".

"You haven't misled me. Anyway, I have no right to ask and you're under no obligation to tell me anything about your personal life—you know that."

"I appreciate your offer."

"I'm selfishly motivated Alex, I assure you. I have to lead by example here. If I've got two PAs it flies in the face of everything the partners are trying to change. I can't have one rule for myself and another rule for everyone else. Normally it wouldn't be a problem to cut back but with you..." JP stopped abruptly in mid-sentence. He didn't want Alex to know the problem he was having was not solely employment related.

"With me ... what?" Alex pressed.

"Never mind."

Over a week passed.

JP didn't broach the topic of Alex's career again. In fact she began to wonder whether he'd forgotten about it. Perhaps he'd even had a change of heart.

Alex heartily wished she could forget it.

The problem was that JP had planted a seed in her mind and tentative imaginings about becoming a lawyer had been plaguing her ruthlessly ever since. Countless times during the week she'd caught herself daydreaming about sitting in lecture theatres, wading through legal books and even making some university friends. Suddenly her dreams had burst out of the confines of her private Alex Farrer world and into the streaming sunlight of JP's hopes and expectations.

But Alex knew it wasn't just the law that appealed to her. It ran deeper than that. It wouldn't have mattered what she did, whether it was an Assistant Legal PA or a High Court justice. What she really yearned for was variety in her life: failures and successes, highs and lows, and vibrant, colourful people. Suddenly JP had lowered a ladder of future possibilities down to her. Now she ached to place her foot on the first rung and begin to climb. But despite what she'd said to JP about the weight of global family expectation there was one mountain of resistance which would be more insurmountable than all the others: Simon.

Simon would *not* like the idea of her doing further study one little bit. He had plans for them and she'd gone along with those plans for so long that any alternative would be like a bolt of lightning out of the blue.

Nevertheless, JP's words had filled her with hope. He was right wasn't he? When you loved someone you supported that person in achieving their dreams. Perhaps she'd underestimated Simon. Perhaps he'd be happy to be talked around to her point of view. All she had to do was explain that their plans for parenthood wouldn't be derailed, just postponed for a few years.

Yet despite talking to Simon on the phone every other day, Alex had struggled to find the right moment to raise the subject with him. It would simply have to wait until they were face to face. Then she could make him understand how important JP's offer was to her.

And so she dreamed and stewed and prayed that JP wouldn't raise the issue again until the road with Simon lay clear. Meanwhile JP swept in and out of the office day after day like a shifting tornado.

He was beside himself with work. Endless streams of emails with long attachments were toppling into his inbox by the hour. Client requests for appointments had blown out to six weeks. She and Vera were both flat out trying to keep on top of his practice commitments. The little spare time he had to discuss anything with them at the end of the day, if he even turned up at the end of the day, was complicating the whole process too.

When he did manage to find a few minutes to go through matters with her Alex was staggered at his ability to focus on one pebble at a time when a whole cliff-face of boulders was coming down on top of him. But business was the strict order of the day whenever they were together. Never again did he allow their discussions to get close to personal. And she certainly wasn't expecting the call from him that came in late one evening as she was packing up for the day.

"I want you to come somewhere with me, on your way home. I'm illegally parked outside the building so you'll have to hurry."

"Where?"

"I'm doing a couple of hours in a community legal centre tonight. I used to volunteer there when I was living here years ago."

Alex bit her lip. "I shouldn't. I'm having dinner with my parents tonight."

"What time are you due there?"

"Seven-thirty."

"I'll have you there by then. I can drop you off. No problem."

"You don't even know where they live." She smiled at his easy resolution of all obstacles.

"Where do they live?"

"Inner West."

"I can get you there. Come on, come with me. You'll see how the little people need the law as much as the corporate giants."

Alex hesitated but the problem was she desperately wanted to go and see how a community centre worked. Everything at Griffen Murphy Lawyers catered for wealthy clients and she often wondered about the people who couldn't afford to pay their senior lawyers over five hundred dollars an hour—who looked after them?

It was not ideal that she'd be alone with JP but how hard could it be to maintain a professional distance, just as they had over the last week? Then in a couple of hours she'd be at her parents' house and it would all be over.

"Okay. I'll go with you. I'd really like to."

"I thought you would. Hurry up then."

Within twenty minutes of climbing into the passenger's seat JP was pulling into a side street of the city's southern outskirts and parking the car. Alex got out and looked around. They were in the middle of one of the most socially disadvantaged areas of the inner city. The legal centre they stood in front of was no more than a run-down shop front.

"What's up?" JP asked as he came around the car to meet her on the footpath.

"I wasn't expecting this."

"What were you expecting? Griffen Murphy Lawyers?" he teased, his mouth lapsing into an amused grin.

"No," she laughed. "But a little more than this."

"These places run on the smell of an oily rag. If volunteers didn't man the joint it wouldn't open. There's some funding but it's meager. Are you ready?"

Alex nodded. JP wandered into the centre to greet a woman behind the front reception desk.

"Jonathan McKenzie!" she screamed, and lifting her wiry physique out of her chair ran into the reception area to throw her arms around his neck. "You've come back to us."

"Couldn't keep away, Marie."

"So they finally let you escape their clutches in London, eh?"

"I couldn't stand another winter there if you want the truth. Marie, I'd like you to meet Alex Farrer. She's my PA."

"Alex, really nice to meet you," Marie cried again, turning on Alex and pumping her hand vigorously for a few seconds, her mass of tight black curls bobbing around her intelligent, fine boned face. "If you're working with Jonathan you'll need nerves of steel."

Alex couldn't help smiling in delight at the irresistible Marie. She clearly adored JP and didn't care who knew it. And reading Alex's expression JP gave her a wink out of Marie's eyeshot, yet he had no idea his tiny gesture was like a blow to her heart.

"So are you back to stay?" Marie pressed.

"At this stage."

"Now don't go committing yourself, will you," she teased. "You're a hard one to pin down. Although I hear a certain English princess by the name of Caroline almost managed to do it."

Almost imperceptibly JP flashed his eyes at Alex before switching them away. But his glance had not been fleeting enough to stop Alex nose-diving into burning curiosity about the mysterious Caroline, mentioned once again as an important part of JP's life.

Marie and JP chatted about the centre, its funding position, who'd moved on and who was still there. Meanwhile, a handful of lone individuals wandered in uncertainly; Marie would smile acknowledgement and ask each one to take a seat in the waiting area. JP asked Marie whether it would be all right if Alex sat in on the appointments.

"Yes, no worries at all. I'll clear it with the punters first. If they have any issues Alex can come out and have a cuppa with me."

There was no need for a cuppa though. None of the clients objected to Alex sitting in on the interviews. And for the next two hours she sat next to JP, transfixed as he probed, questioned, advised, lectured and reassured.

Sometimes he would give them legal advice or dictate letters and file notes for the day solicitors to follow through on. But mostly he spent his time skillfully drilling down to the client's core problems, and often their problems had very little to do with the law.

Alex was impressed. JP's extraordinary gift for dealing with his staff at Griffen Murphy spilled over into his dealings with the clients at the legal centre too. He was able to put them at ease at once, meet them on their own level and give them advice in a way they were sure to be able to understand and take away with them. In fact he was so natural she was sure the clients had no idea they'd just received advice from one of the country's top litigation lawyers.

Alex was still pondering that professional side to JP as she sat beside him in his car. He was heading in the general direction of her parents' suburb according to her directions but at that moment he turned and caught her looking at him.

"What's up?" he asked gently.

"That was an amazing experience. Thanks so much for taking me."

"No problem."

"You don't really understand how bad things can get for some people until they start telling you their stories."

"And unless you're their lawyer or their priest you're not likely to hear those stories anyway."

"But the legal issues were often quite small compared to the rest of their problems."

"That's the way it is, whether it's a mum and dad type client or a large corporation. The legal issues always have to be taken in context. If you deal with them in isolation you can do a lot of damage."

"You were great with those people. You really helped."

JP gave out a loud guffaw.

"What?"

"I've hardly helped them at all. Those poor individuals are so plagued by debt, addictions and violence that nothing I do will have a lasting impact upon them. All you can do is offer them a way forward in the hope they won't do something rash instead."

"That's very cynical."

"Not cynical, just realistic. You've been cosseted like a princess in a tower. You've no idea what real hardship is."

"Just because I've never experienced hardship doesn't mean I don't care about people who have."

"I know that. If you didn't care you wouldn't have been social justice captain at school. But it can't end there. You're out in the big, bad world now and following up on those early instincts is more important than ever. Take Marie for instance. She was the medalist in her year at law school and could have written her own job description in any law firm in the country. Instead she's sacrificed a huge salary because she wants to help people in trouble."

"What are you suggesting? That everyone should be helping the poor and down-and-outs on a full time basis?"

"Of course not. That'd be counterproductive. The best thing for the poor in any country is a strong economy fueled by business and backed up with a strong education and social security system."

"So what *are* you suggesting then?"

"Nothing in particular."

"Yes you are. These comments are directed at me, aren't they?"

"Should they be?"

"Why are you being so cryptic?" Alex snapped, feeling irritated and undermined. He was goading her and she guessed it was over her resistance to the paralegal offer.

"If you have gifts you should be worn out by using them all up by the end of your life," JP declared stridently. "They shouldn't be put in a box and shoved to the back of the cupboard like an unwanted wedding present."

"There are lots of ways people can contribute. Are you suggesting women who stay at home and raise children are wasting their gifts?"

"Of course not. My own mother stayed at home. Raising a family's incredibly important. But for some women there has to be more."

"It's easy for a man to say. Men are still expected to take on the role of full time breadwinners while women are expected to manage paid work as well as a family. It's like having two full-time jobs at once."

"That's true but it can be done. There are openings for part-time work now. One of our lawyers came to me yesterday and asked if she could drop back to part-time to spend more time at home. We're going to team her up with another part-timer in a job share."

"Mmm," Alex murmured thoughtfully, "I wonder whether you'll be feeling as socially progressive when your working wife's getting home late, the dinner's not on, the homework's not done and there are no clean socks. Turn right here. It's just down there on the left near the big tree."

JP laughed at her grim picture of his domestic future. "Nevertheless, when I get married I hope I'll support my wife in her choices and I mean practical support, not just moral support."

"Even when your toddler's spraying baby food all over your two thousand dollar business suit from the high chair?"

JP swung into the kerb and switched off the ignition before turning to her.

"You know, for a princess in a tower you have surprising flashes of insight into the real world sometimes. Speaking of the real world, have you made a decision about my offer yet?"

Alex couldn't answer. His closeness was doing her head in again. And she'd been so sure she was past that; so sure his knowing about her engagement would corral those renegade feelings she'd battled during their first meetings.

"JP ... I can't..." she began but couldn't go on because he was groaning in exasperation and running his hand through his hair. He threw himself back against his car seat and stared blindly out the windscreen, his jaw set rigid. But then he was turning to her again, his voice barely audible.

"Before you say anything more Alex, I want to tell you a story. Will you listen?"

Alex nodded, relieved she wouldn't have to say anything more to defend her decision straight away.

"An oncology nurse, Annabelle, worked in a Glasgow hospital about fifteen years ago. She'd married very young and by that stage had a teenage son but she was still young in mind and body and incredibly bright and beautiful. She was passionate about her work and kept herself up to date with medical developments in fighting the cancers her patients were battling. The medical doctors on staff noticed her as a nurse who showed great promise academically and they encouraged her to think about studying medicine at university and becoming a doctor. She was incredibly excited about this Alex, it had been a dream of hers for a long time—one she'd never believed would come true. All she'd needed was some encouragement and support to start to believe in herself."

"So did she do it?" Alex asked feeling strangely on tenterhooks as JP related his simple story. "Did she become a doctor?"

"I remember the night she came in through the door and I knew something incredible had happened to her that day. I'd never..."

JP stopped then, gazing out over Alex's left shoulder, looking lost and alone as though he'd forgotten she was sitting right next to him.

"You'd never what?" Alex prompted and JP's gaze returned to hers.

"I'd never seen her look so happy. Anyway," JP sighed before he went on, "she made the announcement to my Da and I'll never forget his reaction—jealousy, possessiveness, anger—every ugly motive you can think of within a marriage was going through his head. He'd always been a miserable, violent bully Alex, from as early on as I could remember. But that night she was so goddamn happy that not even *he* could bring her down."

"What happened?" Alex asked, feeling a veil of portentousness wrapping around them both as they sat together in the quiet hush of his car.

"He didn't hurt her that night, not physically anyway, but with the most violent psychological thrashing he could give her he told her she would not get one cent of financial support from him if she went to university. He then walked out of the kitchen, sat himself down on his lounge chair and turned the TV on and the subject never came up again."

"That's a terrible ending," she whispered, swallowing in an effort to get the words out of her choked up throat. "And you?" Alex began again quietly. "Did he beat you too?"

"Oh no," JP replied with a scoff in his voice. "My Da was solid gold coward. He only hit defenseless women; he had enough brains to work out that one day I might be able to throw a major punch back at him. And he wasn't the only one to work that out because at fifteen I started lifting weights and pretty soon I was twice his size."

"And Annabelle?"

"Once I could take him on the beatings stopped but I stayed at home for a few more years, for her sake. I tried to talk her into going to the police, leaving him; you name it, I tried it. But she wouldn't do it. As for becoming a doctor my Da had killed the dream within her as surely as if he'd strangled it with his bare hands. She waited on him for five years until she died within three weeks of being diagnosed with pancreatic cancer."

"And your father?"

"Don't know. Don't care. I haven't spoken to him in over ten years."

"I don't understand, why didn't he want her to study medicine?" Alex was confused at a level that went way beyond the simple story he'd just recounted to her.

"It was all about control. People might dress it up as something else but that's all it comes down to—one person wanting to commandeer another's life."

Alex dropped her eyes and began to fidget with the ends of her hair lying across her shoulder.

"I know my mother's situation was extreme, and I'm certainly not suggesting anyone in your family is a bully. But I do know something about regret and I'm here to tell you: don't do deals with it, Alex. It will eat your life away from the inside out. In my mother's case it ended up killing her."

He'd dropped his head in front of her so that he could see her better in the dim light of his car, bringing his face closer to hers.

"I understand how bitter you are about your father JP, I really do. But you can't be sure that what he did to your mother was the cause of her cancer. Thinking that way will only end in misery for you."

"There's not a doubt in my mind that the two are connected."

She didn't reply as she studied the hard, male angles of his face and the unrelenting light emanating from deep within his dark eyes. Suddenly a hand was cupping that face and drawing it closer to hers. In a haze, she recognised the silver watch around the slim wrist in front of her but it took several more seconds to register that the silver watch, the wrist and that hand were hers.

In the next moment that same wrist was resting on her lap, enclosed in his firm grip.

"If you ever kiss me Alex, I can promise you it won't be out of pity."

"I was *not* going to kiss you!"

JP guffawed. "I've been kissed by enough women in my life to know when it's about to happen *and* when it's their idea."

"That's it, I'm going!" Alex snapped at JP with sharp, shocked finality, horrified at the intimacy of the gesture she'd just shown him—not even wanting to think about what she might have instigated straight afterwards.

"Wait a second. Alex!" JP objected as he firmed his grip around her wrist to prevent her from opening the car door and fleeing into the night. "Can I come in and meet your parents?"

She gawked at him in disbelief. "No way! That's a terrible idea!"

"Why? Will I embarrass you?" he asked with a provocative smile playing at the corners of his mouth as he released her arm.

"I don't want to take you in there," Alex answered in exasperation. "And what's more, I don't want to be cross-examined by you about why not."

JP gave out a short laugh. "Okay. But you haven't answered my question yet."

"About what?" she threw back, completely flustered. She was still trying to work out how she could have reached out and touched him like that without even knowing she was doing it? And was he right about the kiss thing? She didn't think so, but a niggling doubt was eating away at her even as she denied it to herself.

What kind of strange power did JP hold over her? Whatever it was there was one thing she knew for sure. She had to get out of reach of that power as soon as possible before she did something much more serious than caress his cheek.

"I want an answer about the paralegal offer—now."

Alex felt herself slump as she dropped her face into her hands but JP wasn't having a bar of it. Taking each of her hands in his he prised them away.

"Look at me Alex, straight in the eye and give me a straight answer," he demanded.

"I'm going to talk to Simon but I have to be honest JP, I can't see how your offer will work for us." She was surprised at the steady calm underpinning her voice. "I appreciate what you've tried to do but the bottom line is that Simon and I made plans long ago. As I said before, I won't make everyone I love unhappy by turning all those plans upside down now."

JP stared at her in outraged disbelief. "So if you're diagnosed with a terminal illness tomorrow and a month later they find a cure would that be your response? Sorry Doc, Simon and I have made too many plans towards my own demise—hold on to your cure because I refuse to turn things around now?"

"This is not about a terminal illness! This is my life and my choices are going to affect other people, not just myself!"

"Goddamn it! I wash my hands of this!" JP declared and tossed his hands up in the air for emphasis.

"I wish you would wash your hands of this!" Alex countered immediately in hot rebuke. "I never asked you to involve yourself in my life in the first place."

With that she grabbed her bag from the floor of the car, wrestled with the unfamiliar door handle to get it to open and in the next moment was rushing down the footpath towards the safe haven of her parents' home.

Chapter Six

"Are you sure you're all right, Alex?" her mother asked again as she led her daughter down the hallway of her childhood home.

"Yes Mum, I'm fine," Alex assured her, hoping she didn't sound too flustered or dismissive.

"You're very flushed. I think you're working too hard. And you're very thin. Why don't you come back and live at home and I'll fatten you up."

"Stop fussing woman!" Alex's father piped up good-humouredly from his usual position on the sofa in front of the TV.

Alex bent over to peck him on the cheek and he gave her hand an affectionate squeeze.

"I don't need fattening up, Mum."

"Yes Mary, the girl looks fine," Peter Farrer interjected again. "And perhaps you should be checking with her future husband whether he wants her fattened up. You know how much wedding dress fabric costs."

Alex smiled weakly despite the disheveled state of her emotions after fleeing JP's car just minutes before.

Her elderly parents had been engaging in their affectionate banter for as long as she could remember. Being amidst it made her feel warm, safe and secure, as though she was a little girl again. But at the same time her stomach was lurching at their reference to Simon and the wedding, hot knives of guilt over her burgeoning feelings for JP slicing mercilessly through her.

"How's work? You have a new boss, don't you?" Mary Farrer asked as she returned to the cooker to stir the steaming, aromatic contents of her French Ovens.

"Yes, and work's fine thanks," Alex answered as heat filled her cheeks.

"I hope he's treating you properly."

"Yes, Mum."

"Who does he think he is working you back so late?" her father shouted across the room. He was a little deaf and so felt that by shouting himself he would assist everyone else's hearing as well. "Your mother tells me he's had you working in some God forsaken place for hours."

"It was a legal centre."

"Well what do you want to be going and doing there? Do they pay you?"

"No, Dad. The centre provides free legal advice."

"Free! Holy Mary and Joseph! Now I've heard everything," Peter Farrer shouted again from his chair. "Free legal advice! Why haven't I ever had free legal advice?"

"Because you can afford to pay for it. Those people are desperate."

"Afford it! I could afford it until the first lawyer got a hold of me. I've been broke ever since."

"You have the first dollar you ever earned and you know it," Alex replied as she perched on the arm of his lounge chair and draped her arm around his shoulders affectionately.

"Well, you're a good girl," he replied, immediately soothed by her gentle touch. "But you know I'm not happy you're working with lawyers. They're all thieves!"

"Not all of them, Dad. You know you're exaggerating."

"Never trust a man who hasn't produced something you can touch at the end of his working day."

"Lawyers produce words," Alex argued. "And words are important too. Think where we would be today without words."

"A whole lot better off. There was a time when a man's word was as good as his handshake, then someone invented lawyers to complicate things. I tell you, law is no way to make a living."

At that moment the doorbell rang and Alex got to her feet to answer it.

"Sit down girl. A young lady doesn't answer the door at this time of night."

With that, Peter Farrer climbed laboriously out of his chair onto his weak knees and shuffled off down the hallway. Alex wandered over to the cooker to stand beside her mother as she stirred and added to her pots.

The smells that emanated from Mary Farrer's kitchen were always delectable and she cooked gourmet delights at every meal. Alex had just tasted a mouthful of the night's meal off a teaspoon offered by her mother when she was grabbed from behind. She jumped violently, her nerves still on edge after her encounter with JP in the car, before twisting around in a pair of all-encompassing arms.

"Simon!" she whispered breathlessly as she felt the blood drain from her face.

"Surprised?" he asked gleefully, his dark eyes shining with delight.

"Yes ... yes ... I'm staggered. I was only talking to you a few hours ago in New Zealand."

"I know, I rang your Mum from the airport to let her know I'd come straight here. I wanted to surprise you."

"Well aren't you going to give your future husband a kiss?" Mary Farrer prompted with more than a hint in her tone.

"Yes, of course," Alex agreed hurriedly, feeling awkward with her parents in the room.

Simon's mouth descended upon hers for a short hard kiss but then Alex sensed that someone other than her parents was watching them closely.

It was her cousin Monique, standing quietly in the background as she watched the reunion unfold before her.

"Did you and Monique arrive together?" Alex asked Simon in surprise and he nodded, releasing her from his arms.

"Hello, you!" Alex said in delight and moved across the room to hug her cousin. "I had no idea you and Simon were travelling home together. I thought you were still in New Zealand."

"I was," Monique explained. "But I decided to change my flight so that I could come home with Simon."

"Well you look great. Have you had a lovely time?"

"Yes, wonderful. You haven't been to New Zealand have you?" Monique hooked her arm in Alex's and led her away from the family.

"No, I haven't."

"I can't believe that in all the time Simon's been there you didn't manage to get there yourself."

"It's been hard to get away from work. You know how it is."

"Yes, I know," Monique agreed and then lowered her voice a little so that only Alex could hear. "I hope you don't mind that I linked up with Simon for the trip home. I really hate taking flights by myself. The take-offs scare me half to death."

"Of course not," Alex assured her. "I'm glad you both had the company. Simon told me you cooked for him. He would have loved that. You know how he hates any meals which are shop bought."

"That's the least I could do after he'd shown me around Auckland for a whole day."

"Well now you are making me feel guilty," Alex confessed. "I must try and get over there for his next trip." With that Alex looked over at Simon who had his sharp eyes firmly fixed on the two girls. As he heard Alex's last words he wandered over to her and slid his arms around her waist.

"I'm afraid there won't be any more opportunities for you to go to New Zealand, unless we want to go for fun."

"What do you mean?" Alex asked as her heart began to pound away in her chest.

"I've sold the whole business."

Alex gaped at him, dumbfounded. "What? But I thought you were only going to sell part of it."

"They made me an offer. I've jettisoned the whole business. And that means..." he began suggestively, raising his eyebrows.

"You can come back to Australia for good," Alex finished, plastering a smile on her face, waiting for the inevitable upshot of his news.

"And that means you and I don't have to wait any longer to get married. Let's book the church and do it."

Alex nodded in response to his ecstatic look. "Yes ... yes, of course."

Simon's smile dissolved. "You don't look as happy as I expected you would."

"No, I am happy Si, really." Alex reassured him and summoned everything she could from within herself to reflect his own happiness.

But then Alex's eyes caught her mother's. Mary Farrer had been watching her future son-in-law and her daughter and she was now staring at Alex with a look of intense disapproval.

Alex felt sick. Did her mother see something that no one else in the room could, something that even she was having trouble recognising?

At that moment the doorbell rang again. Alex jumped into movement, mainly to escape the scrutiny of her mother and fiancé.

Thankfully her father had been unable to hear the bell over the conversation in the kitchen so she had a free run to collect her thoughts and calm her nerves as she made her way down the hallway. It had all been too much, that was for sure. First, those intense minutes in the car with JP, then the big announcement from Simon. Alex wasn't sure she could take much more.

JP heard the sound of heels clicking on a timber floor within before the front door was swung open.

"Oh no!" Alex shook her head in disappointment and disbelief as she took in the sight of him outside her parents' door.

"That's a nice way to greet your boss," JP replied with a sardonic smirk.

He was enjoying surprising her, he couldn't deny it. And to think he could have been sitting in his car and heading for home right then, still fuming over her final decision about the paralegal offer. Yet that was exactly what he'd planned on doing not ten minutes before as he'd drummed his fingers on the wheel and watched her disappear like an apparition into the house opposite.

Then as fate would have it a call from a client had delayed his departure and thank God it had. But for that call he would not have been sitting there when that cab drew in across the road from where he was parked. He would not have watched a couple get out of the cab and remove their suitcases from the boot. He would not have seen that same couple linger on the footpath for several minutes after the cab had driven away, leaning towards one another as they engaged in an intimate conversation before finally heading into the house. And he would not have had an opportunity to decide it was absolutely necessary he get into that house to find out whether the man he'd just watched making body language love to another woman was Alex's fiancé.

The only problem was JP didn't have a single excuse for barging into her parents' home unannounced. It wasn't until he'd racked his brains, come up with no brilliant ideas at all and thrown the car into gear that he finally saw it: Alex's wallet was lying on the floor in front of the passenger's seat. It had obviously fallen out when she'd grabbed her bag and fled just minutes before.

JP sat back in his seat and laughed in mirthless disbelief as he killed the car engine, wondering whether the devil himself might have made that wallet fall out that night.

"I thought you'd have gone by now," Alex hissed back irritably as the initial shock of seeing him on her parents' doorstep subsided.

"I took a business call after you got out of the car," he explained, loving the effect he was having upon her.

Turning to check no one had followed her down the hallway, Alex pulled the front door closed behind her and stepped out onto the front porch.

"You can't come in," she directed, her voice pitched at near hysteria.

"Why not?" JP drawled, unmoved by her panic.

"You know why not."

"Is it because Simon has arrived? I saw him get out of the cab, you know. I guessed it was him with that pretty little curly haired number."

"That pretty little curly haired number is my cousin, if you must know."

"They make a cute couple," he couldn't resist adding, wanting to see Alex's reaction so that he could gauge whether she had any inkling of what he'd thought he'd seen pass between her fiancé and cousin.

"What do you mean by that?" she asked, visibly perturbed.

"Nothing at all."

"Anyway, you can't come in."

"You know that's very bad manners," he laughed. "And you may want to reconsider your decision not to let me in because I have your wallet."

With that he whipped it out from behind his back to reveal it to her ever so briefly before stowing it away again.

"Give me that!"

"Not until you invite me in," he replied with a grin. He hadn't seen much of Alex's feisty side and he decided he liked it—very much.

"Never!" she cried and launched herself at him, lunging around his powerful physique to grab at the wallet but he was too quick for her. He soon had his arm stretched upwards as she jumped a couple of times to snatch it. But he held it just out of her reach, laughing uproariously the whole time.

"Alex, what's going on?"

At that moment, Alex was airborne in an effort to regain her wallet when the bone chilling tone of a woman's voice reached JP's ears. Alex regained her footing and throwing a silencing look at him swung around to face a dark-eyed, slightly built woman standing in the doorway. She was clearly nonplussed at the shenanigans going on in her garden.

"Mum!" Alex breathed, but then despite her mouth being open to speak, no sound came out.

"It's my fault, Mrs Farrer." JP stepped into the light. "I'm Jonathan McKenzie, Alex's boss."

"Oh!" Mrs Farrer replied, taken aback at JP's ready command of the situation.

"Alex left her wallet in my car. I was just torturing her a little before I gave it back. I didn't mean to interrupt your gathering." With that, he held his hand out to Alex's mother who accepted it, looking a little dumbstruck at his appealing demeanour.

"That's all right, I suppose," she replied doubtfully as Alex watched her in fascination, clearly shocked at her mother's docile acceptance of his explanation. "Won't you come in?"

"No!" Alex cried with a shrill note in her voice. "JP has another commitment."

"JP?" Mrs Farrer questioned, looking hard at Alex and then at him.

"Jon Paul, like the popes," he grinned but the levity was lost on Alex's mother who was completely poker-faced. "And unfortunately my other commitment was cancelled," he added, throwing Alex a look of mock disappointment.

"Well then, come in and have dinner with us," Alex's mother commanded rather than asked.

"Mum's mission in life is to feed the men of the world as often and as much as possible," Alex threw in dryly, looking in grim resignation at her mother.

"Don't be cheeky young lady!" Mrs Farrer scolded but JP could see the affectionate sparkle in her eye as she waggled her finger at her daughter. "You're not too old to be sent to your room, you know."

"I'd love to join you but I wouldn't want to intrude," JP checked insincerely as he raised his eyebrows at Alex provocatively.

"You're not. We're just sitting down at the table now," Mrs Farrer assured him and turning her back on her daughter she made sure to usher JP into the house ahead of her.

Mary Farrer had soon introduced JP to everyone and after accepting a glass of wine he wandered over towards the dinner table. Sensing Alex was deliberately setting out to sit as far from him as possible he changed course like a flash to slip into the seat next to her. By that time all the other table positions had been taken—she had no choice but to remain where she was.

"So you're a lawyer?" Peter Farrer lead the conversation from the head of the table, his voice loaded with scepticism.

JP felt Alex tense at his side. She knew what was coming, as did he. That particular opening from strangers had been landed on him all his professional life. Peter Farrer didn't like lawyers and he was about to let JP know that in no uncertain terms.

"That's right," JP replied brightly, turning to thank Mary Farrer as she loaded his plate with three different kinds of steaming hot meat and vegetable dishes that he didn't recognise but which smelt incredible.

"And you're a partner, yes?"

"Yes."

"So how much do you charge an hour?"

"Dad!" Alex protested. "That's no question to ask at the dinner table."

"Your daughter is right, Peter," Mary Farrer interjected as she took her place at the other end of the table.

JP spoke up anyway. "I don't mind giving Peter an answer to his question if no one else minds hearing it. I charge eight hundred dollars an hour."

"No!" Peter Farrer protested, staring at JP with sharp brown eyes.

"How can you justify that?" Simon asked, shifting his look between JP and Alex from across the table and then JP sensed Alex lower her gaze to her plate.

"Easy," JP remarked casually, "That's market price. If clients want the best litigation practice in town then they have to pay for it."

"But are you the best?" Simon pressed scornfully. "How do your clients know you're better than the next lawyer charging half that?"

"We're not always better but we always get it right. Clients will pay a premium to know their lawyers are getting it right."

"How can you lie straight in bed knowing you're crippling ordinary people with your fees?" Simon shot back with barely concealed hostility.

"We don't act for ordinary people. We act for institutional clients and multi-nationals—although I also have a handful of very wealthy private clients. If a mum and dad matter comes in we refer it out. They can't afford us."

"But eight hundred dollars an hour!" Simon scoffed. "That's a joke!"

"Let me put it this way," JP persisted. "You're in the rag trade, aren't you Simon? The amount of clothing you produce can be almost limitless because no doubt you manufacture off shore. Lawyers can't do that. We're always labour intensive. Although I have lawyers working for me, at the end of the day the clients look to me, as the partner, to give them the cold hard facts about their court case. You make your profits in mass production. I make mine out of intensive services, like a heart surgeon."

"Hah!" Peter Farrer half laughed and half scoffed from the other end of the table. "If I could afford eight hundred dollars an hour I'd hire you Mr. McKenzie. You're the most persuasive man I've ever met." And with that announcement he laughed again. Mary Farrer and Monique smiled uncertainly.

"How many lawyers you got?" Peter Farrer went on.

"Twenty-six in my section."

"And they're all men?"

JP suddenly feared he might choke on his meal. He cleared his throat as he lowered his knife and fork to his plate, wondering whether he may have travelled back in time to the nineteen-fifties.

"More than half my lawyers are women," he explained quietly to the table when he was able to speak again.

"No way!" Simon argued.

"It's true," JP explained suspecting that although he moved in a modern world, in certain quarters people had not changed their attitudes much at all. "Girls have outnumbered the boys in law schools for a long time now. It's a simple equation: if we want the best we have to hire women otherwise we'd end up with second rate lawyers."

"But how does a woman raise a family when she's a lawyer?" Mary Farrer asked in disbelief at what she was hearing.

"That's a good point, Mrs Farrer. It's one that my partners and I are still trying to address but we have a flexible working hours policy. I'm also finding that men are taking on more of the domestic duties for their families at home, which is only fair."

"It's a load of politically correct tripe if you ask me," Simon interjected dismissively before addressing the whole table. "I'm sorry. But women and men are not the same and no one will ever convince me that women have the head for law and business that men do."

JP stared at Simon as indignation rose hot within him.

In that single moment he completely got what made Alex tick. But it didn't make him feel satisfied. In fact, although there was something warm and honest about Peter and Mary Farrer, JP felt thoroughly depressed. The stifling attitudes were closing in around him, just as they had for his own mother. He knew then that only an iron will within Alex would ever allow her to become mistress of her own destiny within that environment. He despaired for her.

He opened his mouth to respond to Simon's last comment when the girl herself suddenly slid her hand over his under the table and squeezed it. It took his breath away but it was not an affectionate squeeze. She was sending him a message, begging him to stop, pull back, and not demolish her fiancé in front of all those she loved most in the world, as she knew he could without even trying. JP snapped his mouth shut again, caught her hand firmly in his own and squeezed it hard. 'Trust me', he was saying back to her. For although he didn't want to hurt her he would not back off. There was some excuse for Alex's parents—they were elderly and from an earlier generation—but there was no excuse for Simon. He was a young man living in a modern country. He should know better.

"Simon, I invite you to open the paper any day of the week and read the winding up and bankruptcy notices," JP began chattily. "Not even that. Just open up the business section and read about the latest corporate collapse. Men in their infinite wisdom have placed other men at the head of these operations and men have been presiding over financial disasters since business enterprise began."

Simon opened his mouth to speak but JP would not be interrupted. His hand was unwittingly squeezing Alex's tighter and tighter as he spoke. He was driven by a need to speak up not only for Alex but for his own mother too; for every woman denied the opportunities they deserved.

"In my experience women are much more likely to come in early and seek advice if their business is in trouble," JP argued on. "Men are more inclined to sit back and hope it will all go away. Their pride gets in the way, you see. So they try to crash through."

"Well, there's no way I'd let a female lawyer loose on my business affairs—no matter how clever you say they are," Simon tossed in bitterly, visibly overwhelmed by JP's arguments.

JP's hand still held Alex's tightly but he sensed her squeeze one of his fingers as best she could in his iron grip. In the briefest of glances he told her with his eyes he would pull back and not finish Simon off.

"The most important thing is that the client is comfortable with his lawyer," JP remarked without feeling. "If you're more comfortable with a male lawyer then you should definitely stick with that. I still prefer a male GP for certain medical examinations, needless to say."

At that Peter Farrer threw back his head and laughed out loud. "I like this fellow!" he announced to the table. "Even if he is a lawyer and charges eight hundred dollars an hour."

Across the table Simon took a mouthful of his dinner looking triumphant. His expression said it all: he'd won the argument with the big firm lawyer.

JP could feel Alex relax a little at his side and a twinge of guilt made him hesitate for a split second over what he was about to do, but not for long. If he was going to put the cat amongst the pigeons over Alex's future then now was the time to do it.

"Speaking of female lawyers," JP began chirpily. "Alex here has one of the finest legal brains I've come across." He was met with a stony silence that he ignored, continuing to eat as everyone stared at him.

"Alex?" Peter Farrer queried in disbelief as JP stopped chewing.

"Yes, Alex."

"But she's not a lawyer." Mary Farrer's expression was confused.

"Doesn't matter. She has better natural instincts for the law than some of my qualified lawyers."

"I don't think we need to go into that now," Alex protested, finally yanking her hand out of JP's in fury.

"My Alex is a clever girl. She got good grades in her finals," Peter Farrer announced proudly.

"I know. I've seen her final grades. They were outstanding."

"What are you suggesting Mr McKenzie?" Peter Farrer pressed.

JP looked slowly around the table. Every set of eyes except Alex's was fixed expectantly upon him.

"I've put Alex's name forward to my partners as a student paralegal," he explained, unperturbed by the hard looks he was receiving from Simon. "That means she'd be a law student employed by the firm and she'd receive a generous contribution from us towards her university fees."

You could have cut the air with a knife. Alex was staring down at her plate in despair and JP suspected the night was fast becoming one of the worst of her life.

"Have you started this process, Alex?" Simon asked sharply.

"No, not yet," Alex answered in a shaky voice. "I said I'd talk to you."

Simon sat upright and threw his napkin down on the table in disgust. JP glanced at Alex to see her blush to her hairline.

"I think this is a subject for another day," Mary Farrer announced in a commanding, no-nonsense voice and JP suspected that when Alex's mother put her foot down, no one crossed her.

The conversation moved on to safer subjects but JP couldn't deny the relief he felt when he finally got to his feet after coffee and explained he would have to head off.

He farewelled everyone, trying to catch Alex's eye, but it was useless. She was determined not to look at him. Out of courtesy he asked if he could drive anyone home. There was a silence as everyone looked at each other.

"I said I'd drop Monique home," Simon explained awkwardly, looking at Alex with an odd mixture of desire and uncertainty.

"No Simon, you take Alex home. I'll get a cab," Monique offered

"No Monique, you're on the way home to Simon's in the south. I'll get a cab," Alex interjected.

"I'll take everyone home!" Peter Farrer dropped in.

"No old man, you'll do no such thing," Mary Farrer protested. "You've had too many scotches."

"Look," JP stepped in, sensing an opportunity, "This is silly. Alex and I are going north and Simon and Monique are going south. I'll drop Alex home. That's the only sensible thing to do."

The debate raged for another minute but then everyone accepted that JP's suggestion was the right one. Goodbyes were said and JP was left smouldering with a rare attack of jealousy as Simon took Alex in his arms.

"Can we talk tomorrow?" JP heard Simon ask her, more conciliatory now than when he'd first heard her news about the paralegal program.

"Of course," Alex replied as she appeared to be trying to placate him with her eyes.

But there was nothing placatory about Alex in his car. She sat rigid and angry—so furious she was unable to speak. JP was unwilling to broach any subject either and the entire journey was undertaken in a heavy silence.

In monosyllables Alex directed him to her home and he complied without response. When finally he slid the car into the kerb he turned off the engine and swung around in her direction.

"Okay. Get it off your chest," he commanded in a bland voice. "You've obviously got something to say."

She turned to face him, her eyes huge in the dim light of the car, her voice shaking with anger.

"I do have some things I want to say. I want to tell you exactly how I'm feeling and what I'm thinking and then I never want to have another conversation like this ever again. I want you to stay out of my private life. What you said tonight at the dinner table about the paralegal program was more damaging than you can ever begin to imagine. Are you trying to emasculate my fiancé in front of everyone he loves? Simon and I have made our own plans for the future and you shouldn't interfere with them. I like ... no, I'm going to be dead honest with you tonight on every level. I love working with you JP. You make me feel as though I can do anything—be anybody. I don't want to leave you ... I mean my job, but ... whenever you're around I can't think straight ... I have to stop that happening..."

"Alex..." JP interrupted as he reached out a hand to touch her cheek as the fiercest, most compelling desire he'd ever felt for a woman raged within him, but she switched back as though avoiding a slap.

"No! That's what I mean. That's the second time tonight something like that has happened. We mustn't ever touch each other again."

JP watched her in the half-light. He was losing her again. The brick wall was going up; just as it had the evening he'd offered her the paralegal job.

"Is there a point coming anytime soon?" he demanded in frustration.

"The point is that if we can't keep a formal distance from one another then I'll have to go. If you've got to get rid of a PA then I understand it has to be me.

Don't put this paralegal thing in place just to fix the surplus staff problem you have."

"That's not what it's about. Do you think I'd cook that up at the expense of my own firm, just to soothe my guilt about getting rid of a PA? You've got the makings of a great lawyer Alex, and that's the bottom line."

"If I asked for a transfer to another partner but still wanted to take up the paralegal grant would you agree to that?"

He looked at Alex as he pondered her question. "I wouldn't be happy about it," he admitted finally.

"You see?" she declared in triumph.

"I need a paralegal, I want you in that role and I don't apologise for it. And if something else is happening between us at a personal level then maybe you should be asking yourself why."

"Don't say things like that."

"You mean the truth?"

"You just don't seem to get it. I'm going to be married soon."

JP scoffed. "You can't marry Simon. Even if I knew we were never going to meet again after tonight I'd still say that to you. Why do you think I went into your parents' house tonight? I saw Simon go in. I guessed who it was and I had to see for myself. You'll be a trophy wife, Alex. That's what he wants."

"No, that's not true."

"It is true. I understand men like Simon better than you think. He'll cherish you as a wife, sure, but only if you do whatever suits his self-image as the head of the household. You can bet your life that's not going to include anything more than family commitments for you."

"But there's nothing wrong with family commitments!"

"I know that!" JP blurted in exasperation. "But you won't have a choice. I understand your background is very different to mine but that won't stop you withering in a marriage where you get no say in deciding anything for yourself. You've got to tell Simon what you really want and if you're content with how he reacts you'll know what to do. And if you do choose him I'll never raise these issues again."

JP knew he was pouring forth in a tirade but he couldn't help it. Alex would never guess the tirade had as much to do with his own mother as it did with her.

"This is not about choosing Simon or you. This has nothing to do with you!" The anguished cadence in her voice hung in the air as silence descended between them. "Don't you see JP? The way you pre-empted what I wanted tonight, announcing to everyone I might be joining the paralegal program—you, Simon, my father—all making plans for me!"

134

"Then tell us what *you* want Alex—tell all of us."

"I will. And you'll see you're wrong about everything. This is my problem, not Simon's. I should have spoken up earlier about what I wanted to do with my life. How can he support my choices when he doesn't know what's going on in my head?"

"Well I sincerely hope he'll be supportive but forgive me if I don't crack open the champagne just yet."

"You see? You're doing it again."

"Doing what?"

"Declaring how things are going to be before I've had a chance to find my own way. You're so critical of Simon but don't you see that you're exactly like him? Do you have any idea how discouraging it is if those you love hand down the blueprints for your life before you've had a chance to work out what you want yourself?"

"Is that what you think I'm doing?" JP asked in disbelief but at the same time wondering whether including him as someone she loved had been an error or a truthful slip. "You think I'm forcing you in a certain direction?"

"Of course you are. Even though we've only just met I feel as though I'm being pulled apart in a tug of war. You're just as determined as Simon that I do things your way."

JP sat back in his seat and stared out through the windscreen. Was she right? Was he no better than Simon? Was he browbeating her into submission just like everyone else in her life—just like his own father had bullied his own mother into a never-ending torpor of unhappiness and submission?

Taking a deep breath he let it go slowly. He had to pull back for he was beginning to care about Alex, more than he dared to admit. But if he cared about her he had to give her the space she needed to find her own way, otherwise she'd end up resenting him as just another browbeater in her life.

After a minute he turned to her again. "Is that what you want, Alex? You want me to back off from you and your life, in every way?"

She nodded.

He pressed his lips together in a hard grimace. He was worried that by backing off he might lose her. But the alternative, forcing his way into her life and trying to run it for her was no longer an option if he wanted her to become a part of his life. And that was precisely what he did want.

He'd been prepared to back off from her when she'd told him about the engagement, but his time with Simon and her family that night had given him a clear view of what lay in store for her, and he didn't like it. He hadn't quite gotten to the bottom of whatever was going on between Simon and Alex's cousin but what he did know was that Alex was headed straight for the ornamental mantelpiece in her fiancé's life.

He would have to tread carefully though. He knew what his own temperament could be: demanding, impatient, willful. It would take every ounce of his self-control to give Alex the space she needed so that she didn't dematerialise before him and disappear out of his life forever. She was that fragile.

"Okay then Alex, if that's what you really want," he replied, his mouth taut with determination. "Although you and I may both live to regret this decision."

"It is what I want."

"Then I'll be the model of formal propriety from now on," he confirmed wryly. "And I'll have to get my head around it by next Monday because we're going to be working closely together."

"What does that mean?"

"It means I have a client coming down from Queensland to give me a statement. I'll need you with me from ten in the morning until late, maybe after midnight. No, don't start arguing with me until I've finished. That call I received tonight, just before I arrived at your parents' door, it was from that client. He's developing a resort up north and wants me to commence proceedings against his builder. I need you to come with me to his hotel so that you can type his statement up as we go. We'll only have one day to get it right as he's leaving on Tuesday."

"But why can't he come to the office?"

"Because contrary to my instructions he shipped fifteen boxes of files to the hotel instead of my office. Now that they're there I'm not going to risk any going missing during another move. Between you and me Alex, this guy's as slippery as an eel and I wouldn't put it past him to lose a few reams of paper if it suited his case."

"But can't Vera...?"

JP was already shaking his head. "I'm sorry, if you think I'm taking Vera you can forget it. She's not up to this job, you are."

Alex wrung her hands together in fidget-ridden torment. "It's not the late night, or the hours..." she began to explain.

"I know. It's the two of us together but you don't need to worry Alex, I'll treat you the way I treat any other PA in the firm—just as you want."

Chapter Seven

When Sophie was made Acting Head of HR her brother had given her an illustrated coffee table book featuring the best excuses to give your boss when taking a sickie. When Alex visited Sophie's house she'd occasionally flick through its pages and some of the more creative excuses were still clear in her mind.

'My dog is having a nervous breakdown' was one of Alex's favourites, as was 'My toe is stuck in a bath tap.' There were quite a few others coming to Alex's mind too as she travelled to work that morning. Unfortunately, she was positive that none of them would satisfy JP were she to ring in sick that day, despite their creative flair. But it wasn't until she sat down at her desk at eight-thirty, her mobile phone ringing like crazy in the depths of her handbag, that she finally accepted that her mental quest to find a way out of an entire day sitting next to JP had failed.

"Hi Hun!" Simon piped up cheerfully on the other end of her phone when Alex finally answered it. "Can you get away for an hour by any chance? I'm in the city now. "

Alex hesitated. Normally she wouldn't leave the office for no good reason but she was going to be working very late and so agreed immediately. Somehow, she'd clear it with JP and it would give her an opportunity to spend some desperately needed private time with Simon.

Despite spending most of the weekend together at his family's house things were still strained between them. Time and time again she'd tried to begin a conversation to clear the air after JP's interference at her parents' home. She was also desperate to raise the subject of her working and studying for the next few years rather than starting their family straight away but an opportunity never seemed to come up. In fact, Alex wondered at times whether Simon was intentionally avoiding being alone with her so that he could also avoid discussing the sensitive topics JP had raised.

"Yes, I'm sure I can get away. That'll be fine," she replied. "Where are we going?"

"It's a surprise. I'll pick you up outside your building in ten minutes and have you back in the city by ten."

"Are you sure you can't give me a hint about where we're going?"

"No, so don't ask. See you soon." With that he rang off without giving Alex any further chance to protest.

Feeling oddly unsettled about what lay in store for her that morning she wandered distractedly into JP's office. He was poring over papers at his desk but his blue eyes soon began a slow but detached elevation across every square inch of her body before resting finally upon her face.

"New dress?"

"Yes. My friend Sophie helped me choose it. In fact, who am I kidding? She did choose it." Alex could hear the babble in her voice as she ran a hand nervously over the cool lycra of the navy blue dress that fitted her like a glove before adding, "I'm not much good at that sort of thing."

"Aye, I know that," he agreed, a droll curl at his mouth. "What can I do for you?"

"Do you mind if I go out for about an hour now? I wouldn't normally ask but it's important and I'll be out of action until tomorrow..."

"That's fine," he interrupted. "Where are you going?"

"I don't know. Simon wants to take me somewhere."

JP muttered something inaudible.

"What did you say?" Alex asked tetchily He didn't need to put his two cents worth into it. After all, he'd promised to stay out of her private life.

"Nothing. Are you still free for this ten o'clock meeting with Mark Jackson?"

"Of course. I said I was."

"So you think you'll be coming, even though you're having this rendezvous with Simon this morning?"

"Yes," Alex replied, unable to keep the edginess out of her voice, unsure where he was coming from with his questioning.

"All right then. I'll meet you in the hotel foyer at ten."

Alex wandered back out feeling wretched and unhappy and she had no idea why. Her mood wasn't improved when her mobile rang again and her mother's voice was at the other end.

"Have you got a minute, Alex? I need to speak to you."

Alex's heart sank. She knew that tone of voice. A lecture was on its way.

"I don't really have a minute Mum, no," she replied, but sensing the call was going to go ahead whether she liked it or not she wandered into an empty office nearby and closed the door.

"I'll only be a minute. This can't wait." Mary Farrer's reply was sharp.

Alex sighed. Short of hanging up on her own mother there was no possible way she was going to escape the talk.

"I've hesitated about asking you this until now but it can't wait any longer. I want to know what's going on with you, young lady. Last Thursday night was a three-ring circus. You're supposed to be marrying Simon but anyone looking at you would never have guessed it. I saw the way you looked at Jonathan

McKenzie. The way he looked at you. Do you think I'm blind?"

"I don't know what you mean," Alex said, genuinely shocked at her mother's acute observational powers.

"Oh yes you do. Something's going on there."

"Mum, that's just not right," Alex defended herself, although her mother was breathtakingly closer to the truth than she knew.

"I don't know that Simon saw what I saw but if you carry on like that it'll only be a matter of time."

"There's nothing to see, Mum. I promise you, there's nothing going on."

"You're playing a dangerous game, Alex. I love Monique but I know she's got her eye on Simon. One false move from you and you'll lose him to her for good and who would blame him?"

"How can you suggest that of Monique?" Alex shot back.

Monique pursuing Simon? It couldn't be true!

"Easily. I wasn't born yesterday. She's crazy about him and he's a good catch."

"This is not a fishing competition!" Alex was unable to keep the exasperation out of her voice. Somehow she had to wind the phone call up, and fast.

"That's exactly what it is. And what's all this nonsense about studying law? What do you want to go and do that for when you and Simon are starting a family soon? You'll never use it."

"What if it's what I want," Alex snapped. "Has anyone actually asked me what I want? Have you and Dad once sat me down and asked me what I want to do with my life, my career, my marriage...?" Alex stopped and closed her mouth, wondering where all the pent up anger was coming from all of a sudden.

Silence reigned on the other end of the phone. "Your father and I have done everything for you," Mary Farrer replied eventually in a crackly voice, clearly hurt. "And now you're suggesting that we've forced you into things?"

"No I'm not blaming you and Dad. Things got away from me a long time ago and I should have spoken up sooner. It's my fault."

"I don't understand where all this talk is coming from! Your father and I want whatever makes you happy."

"But I'm not happy Mum, that's the problem," Alex croaked huskily, tears welling. A long silence reigned on the other end of the phone before Alex continued.

"I know you want me to be happy but my life is in a big mess and I don't know how to fix it. I don't know how to start telling the people I love what it is I really want. But I'm sorry, I'm going to have to hang up now. I'm at work and Simon's picking me up soon..."

"All right then," Mary conceded. "I'll let you go but I think you'd better come over soon and talk to your father and me. Can you come tonight?"

"No. I'll be tied up with work until late. I'll give you a call as soon as I can come over."

Alex rang off in a daze of disbelief. Was her mother right? Was there really something between herself and JP? Was Monique really on a mission to lure Simon away from his engagement? Impossible questions! And absolutely no chance to digest them, for Alex had to grab her bag and head out of her office as fast as she could to meet Simon outside.

"Where are we going?" she asked breathlessly just minutes later as she slipped into the passenger seat of Simon's black Saab.

"Bellevue Hill."

"Bellevue Hill!" Alex echoed. What could possibly be at Bellevue Hill that he needed to pull her out of work for? "And you won't let me know what this is all about?"

"No," Simon shook his head definitively. "Do you have to rush back to work? I thought we could grab an early lunch afterwards."

Alex felt a sick feeling in her stomach as she anticipated his reaction to her next response. "I can't,

Simon. I'm sorry. I have to be at the Central Hotel for a meeting at ten. I'm likely to be there until late, maybe after midnight."

"Until when?" he bit back, slamming his hand down upon the steering wheel, unable to conceal his frustration and anger. "Why didn't you tell me about this?"

"I was going to tell you this morning on the phone but you cut me off."

"This is getting ridiculous! When are you going to give up all this nonsense, Alex?"

"It's not nonsense. It's my work."

"Tell them you can't go," he demanded.

"No, I've agreed to go so that a statement can be drawn up today, and it's not an unreasonable request when you work at a law firm. The matter's urgent."

"I can't take too much more of this!" Simon warned. "I could cope with it when I was busy in New Zealand but now I'm back I don't want to be met with your work commitments every time I suggest something."

"I like working Simon, you know that."

"You don't need to work. I'm a wealthy man."

"But I want to work," she argued. How could she put it more simply?

"Maybe I could understand it if you were doing something important. But the way you're talking you'd think you were Hilary goddamn Clinton!"

Alex's hand rose to her lips and pressed on them tightly to stop the violent wobble that threatened. But she couldn't hold back the two salty tears of crushing humiliation stinging her eyes. She stared out the passenger window and brushed them away. She couldn't have said a word if she'd tried. Simon withdrew into a sulky, guilty silence that Alex knew from experience would last quite awhile.

Within fifteen minutes they were pulling up outside an apartment complex. Alex was sufficiently aware of her surroundings to notice it all looked brand new and that a sale board was out the front. Her heart pounded in anxious anticipation.

When they climbed out of the car a man approached them from the front door and held out his hand firstly to Simon and then to Alex.

"Robert Jones. We spoke this morning, Simon. This must be your fiancée. Nice to meet you, Alex."

The blood was pounding so deafeningly at her temples that Alex hardly knew how she babbled a greeting in return. Thankfully, like so many real estate agents, he had the gift of the gab and dominating the conversation he soon had them through the front door of the stunning but rather soulless apartment.

Alex was grateful that Robert kept them fully occupied with his endless pitch about the modern features of the vast property. She wandered around in a half daze, nodding and making admiring noises every now and then. Simon watched her closely but she couldn't bring herself to look at him.

Close to half an hour must have passed as Robert talked the talk. Simon asked lots of questions about proximity to schools, transport and shops. Finally Robert and Simon got around to price and Alex almost fell over.

"We should be able to persuade the developer to come in at under three and a half," Robert explained. "He hasn't been able to offload as quickly as he'd have liked and is under some pressure."

Three and a half million dollars! Alex was staggered. She couldn't help but stare at Simon. She'd known he was comfortable but had no idea he was that well off. Robert was looking at Alex carefully when he suggested that Simon might like to take her out onto the terrace to discuss an offer.

She wandered outside obediently. Each apartment was cantilevered down a steep slope. The apartment they were in was at the top and had stunning views across the eastern suburbs to the distant ocean. A lap pool to their right sparkled aqua blue in the bright sunshine. Adjacent to it was an enormous marble terrace. It was like something on the Amalfi Coast—it was every girl's dream home.

"Well, what do you think?" Simon queried, his expression a mixed offering of excitement and awkwardness after their earlier conversation.

"It's beautiful," Alex murmured as she basked in the warm morning sunshine.

"Can you see yourself living here?"

"Simon, I've never seen myself living in a home like this. I had no idea you could afford it."

"You mean 'we'," he corrected her.

"Whatever. It's a lot to think about. And we haven't looked at anything else yet."

"You won't find better than this."

"Perhaps not, but don't you think it would be a good idea if we looked for a place together? Robert said the developer was having trouble selling these so why don't we take a few weeks and see what's around?"

Simon's features grew hard. "This is all because of the comment I made in the car about your work, isn't it?"

"No, of course not, although I want us to talk more openly about our future from now on. You've been away so long and there's lots we need to discuss."

Simon laughed spitefully. "Like whether or not a three and a half million dollar home is good enough for you?"

Alex flushed as she noticed Robert disappear inside the apartment to give them more privacy.

"It's not that Si," she explained, keeping her voice low. "We should be planning things together. Isn't that half the fun?"

"Fun! This is fun, isn't it? I bring you along to a place like this and suggest we buy it only to be told in the car that you're too busy with work to stay long and you think we should be discussing everything together!"

Alex couldn't answer. Again she was fighting back tears of frustration and misery. But was Simon right? Was she just being difficult?

"I feel as though your work has always been more important to you than our engagement," he railed. "You've resisted everything I've tried to do to move it forward to a wedding."

"You're right, I have," she conceded. "And I'm sorry about that. We were engaged very young and I felt we were far too immature to get married back then. But we can move forward now. There's nothing to stop us."

"Except your work," he corrected, pressing the advantage he sensed he was gaining in their conversation.

"Simon, let's not talk about that again. Not here."

"Why not? It's highly relevant to this discussion. How are you going to plan a wedding when you're working the hours you are?"

"I can do it," she assured him. "Lots of girls in the office juggle both."

"But I don't want you to 'juggle' it. I want you to have time to do it properly rather than just jamming phone calls and menus in at spare moments."

"Are you saying you want me to give work up now?"

"Yes, I guess I am," he declared bluntly. "And you can forget all that nonsense about doing law too. You'll never use it; it's a complete waste of our time and money."

Alex turned away and gazed blindly out across the view, taking in nothing.

"We're going to start a family soon anyway," Simon continued, unmoved by her silence. "We always agreed we would."

"No, Simon," Alex replied coldly, "You agreed we would. I'm far from being ready to start a family."

Alex watched transfixed as his face turned pink with anger. "This is ridiculous," he scoffed, shaking his head. "You're a secretary. You earn a fraction of the profits I'll be taking out of my next business. You'll make no contribution to our financial position at all."

"That's not the point," Alex argued, reeling from his dismissal. "I enjoy it. I enjoy the challenge and the friendships. I enjoy having a shape to my day when I wake up every morning. And I ... I think I'm pretty good at it."

"Okay," Simon announced, suddenly brighter as though thinking a great idea through. "If you really want to work for awhile you can come and be a secretary at my business, part-time."

Alex swallowed. His expression told her he was clearly struck by the sense and logic of his suggestion. How could she explain that it was not enough?

"I don't want to work part-time. And I don't think it's a good idea for a husband and wife to work together anyway."

"This is all because that boss of yours has done a job on your ego about doing law, isn't it?"

"No, that's not fair, Simon. What you don't know is that I've wanted to do law for a long time and certainly before JP arrived. He made the offer, that's true, but my real failure is that I should have discussed it with you and Mum and Dad ages ago. I was wrong not to."

"God help me, all of a sudden you're thinking about no one but yourself!"

"Sorry to interrupt," Robert had approached Alex and Simon without their noticing. He'd clearly heard much of their recent exchange. "I have to show another place shortly but I can meet you back here later today if you'd like to see it again."

"Alex here has to go back to work on a very important job," Simon explained sulkily. "But I'd like to look at it again."

Not another word passed between them as minutes later she and Simon walked to the car.

"I can phone for a cab if that's easier," Alex offered, knowing he would never agree.

"Don't be ridiculous. Get in," he ordered and they were the last words he uttered to her that day.

When he pulled over at the drop-off zone outside the hotel he glared straight ahead through the front windscreen, drumming his fingers on the steering wheel.

"Si, can we please not leave things like this. This is awful," Alex pleaded but he didn't flinch. The second she stepped onto the footpath and closed the car door he sped off in a fury of rubber tyre friction on tarmac.

Alex stood there motionless, watching as his black car weaved recklessly through the long line of cabs and other vehicles in the traffic. In a daze of mortification and heartache she then walked into the foyer of the hotel.

JP was waiting for her.

He was sitting on a lounge chair with one foot propped up on his other leg, balancing his laptop precariously on his knee and typing very badly with only two fingers involved in the process. Alex stood there frozen, almost insensible of what she would do or say to him.

As though sensing her presence he looked up and then straight across at her. His smile was heart meltingly gentle as he shifted his computer onto the seat next to him and climbed to his feet. Watching her closely he walked slowly to where she stood rooted to the ground.

"You came," he murmured quietly, running a hand through his hair in a clear gesture of relief. "I had the strongest feeling you wouldn't; I fully expected to get a call from you at any minute ... what's wrong?"

But before the words had escaped his lips it started.

Great, racking sobs gripped Alex's entire body as she burst into tears. Dropping her bag to the ground she lifted her hands to cover her face and stooped forward under the crushing weight of the agony consuming her. In the next moment, he'd gathered her into his arms as she moaned and sobbed helplessly into the safe haven of his broad chest.

Chapter Eight

Alex didn't take much interest in business. She didn't take much interest in the men and women who ran corporate Australia either. But Mark Jackson was one industry mogul who she had heard of. Who hadn't?

He was the twenty-eighth richest person in the country. More importantly, his story was a rags-to-riches wonder that was regularly splashed across the pages of glossy magazines and newspapers.

He was a man who could take on governments and their laws and win. He loved fast cars, fast boats, fast profits and fast women. Meanwhile, his formidable wife of forty years stayed at home, spent his money and survived every one of her husband's string of high profile mistresses.

Alex was nervous about spending the day with a man as notorious as Mark Jackson, but not so JP.

To the contrary, JP looked perfectly at ease as he sat at the hotel conference table, using the time before his client's arrival to review the papers in preparation of the session stretching ahead of them. Alex was leafing through papers too, trying to get on top of the maze of factual circumstances lying at the heart of the matter. But the raw despair of her meeting with Simon that morning was too fresh to allow her to focus on any one thing for more than a few seconds at a time.

What a disaster! How had she and Simon reached the point where they could hardly communicate? She couldn't see anything his way and he was just as lost with her. Yet she had a frightening feeling that Simon was pretty much what he had always been and that disturbed her more than anything, because if that was true then she was the one who had changed and the fault was all hers.

But had she changed, or was she just vocalising her dreams to an unenthusiastic audience? It felt as though JP was the only one who instinctively recognised her deepest longings, more than she did herself. But how did JP know her so well? And why did she feel more comfortable with him than she did with her own fiancé? It was as though they were...

At that moment a profound revelation danced away beyond Alex's conscious thought like a sprite in the breeze, before vanishing into the deepest recesses of her soul.

She and JP were soon joined by a portly, middle-aged man. He'd clearly been born and bred in the country, going on his tough, leathery complexion. His rasping voice as he greeted Alex was testament to thousands of cigarettes and many more alcoholic drinks. As proof, he had a half-full bottle of scotch in his hand. He explained that a jug of lemonade was on its way for the legal eagles. "Someone has to be alert," he joked before adding a bellicose, rumbling chortle. He then made a shameless study of Alex's breasts before taking up a chair and lighting a cigarette. Mark Jackson had arrived.

Alex wasn't sure when JP had first formed his opinion of Mark Jackson but dislike and distrust oozed from every one of his pores. Yet unperturbed he began to patiently work his way through the convoluted business dealings between Mark and his contracted builder, but it was like pulling teeth.

Alex typed, deleted and re-typed until every muscle in her body was aching but JP never let up. Over and over he would challenge Mark, shoving documents under his nose and asking him to explain each lie and inconsistency he peddled. Ever so slowly the truth was chipped away and revealed but it took hours. Meanwhile, Mark Jackson became more intoxicated and difficult to communicate with. After more than three hours had passed JP finally suggested they all have a break and with that Alex shot to her feet with alacrity, excusing herself to go to the ladies. As soon as she left the room she reached for her phone.

After all those hours of stewing she had to contact Simon and talk about what had happened that morning at the house, for he was right. She had been reluctant to advance the wedding plans and of course he was frustrated and angry about that. Wouldn't any reasonable man feel the same way?

There had to be a way they could work through their issues. She was sure that if they had some time alone, away from a hovering real estate agent, they could resolve everything. Who knew? Perhaps they both wanted the same things but were simply coming at them from different angles.

The fast dial to Simon's mobile soon clicked through but it rang so many times that Alex was gathering her thoughts to leave a message.

"Hello?" A young woman's voice was suddenly on the other end of the line.

"Oh ... I'm sorry," Alex replied. "I've rung the wrong number.'

"Is that you, Alex?"

Suddenly the penny dropped. "Monique?" Alex asked tentatively.

"Yes, it's me."

"What ... what are you doing answering Simon's phone?" Alex blurted before she could stop herself. It sounded accusatory but Alex's pulse was already racing as suspicion rose within her.

"I'm with Simon ... we were just ... I mean ... he wanted me to look at an apartment."

"Which apartment?"

"It's in Bellevue Hill ... Alex, are you there?"

"I'm here," she answered quietly as the reality check seeped through her veins like poison; so her mother was right: Monique did have her sights set on Simon.

"He wanted my views about it from a woman's perspective," Monique explained, the guilt almost oozing out of the phone.

"Could you put Simon on please?" Alex's voice was cool.

"I'm afraid he's talking to the agent outside. Can he call you back in a minute?"

Alex replied stiffly that she was working but that she'd phone him later and then ended the call. Easing herself onto a chair she sat very still and tried to absorb the new turn of events.

So Monique wanted Simon. But did Simon want Monique?

Alex fought hard to sort her thoughts into some kind of rational order. Simon and Monique had clearly spent time alone in New Zealand, and they'd changed their bookings so that they could fly home together. Then there'd been that awkward conversation as Simon had explained he had to drive Monique home the night they'd had dinner at her parents. Come to think of it, he hadn't really resisted very much when JP had wanted to take her home; wouldn't a love struck fiancé do anything to be alone with his girl when they'd been apart for so long—particularly when her attentive new boss seemed eager to step into his shoes?

Was it really possible she'd missed all the signals between Monique and Simon that night at her parents' house when her mother, and perhaps JP too, had not? But who was she kidding? Alex knew she'd been so distracted by JP that night she hadn't been capable of noticing anything.

Alex jumped as her mobile sang into life. She grabbed it and before looking at the screen blurted Simon's name down the line.

"No it's not Simon. It's me," JP answered gruffly. "Where are you?"

"Just down the hall." Alex looked at her watch and realised she'd been gone from the conference room for nearly a quarter of an hour."

"Well if you haven't immersed yourself in some hotel spa treatment do you mind getting back here? I want to start again." He rang off.

Normally JP's curt order would have bothered Alex but not that afternoon. She was too flustered about Monique and Simon to react to JP and yet she knew she shouldn't jump to conclusions about her fiancé and her cousin. It could all be quite innocent, she told herself as she turned off her phone; the last thing she wanted was Simon calling back and launching into an emotionally charged conversation with her in front of JP and Mark Jackson.

"It's about time," JP murmured without looking up as Alex strode back into the conference room.

"I need to talk to you," she demanded hotly.

JP lifted his eyes slowly from his papers to meet hers. "Unless it's about work that's going to be difficult. Mark Jackson will be back in a minute."

"It's about Simon and Monique."

"What about them?" JP asked as he threw his pen down on the table and rose to his feet.

"I need to know what you saw when they got out of the cab last week."

JP stared hard at her. "Why?"

"You said they made a cute couple. I need to know whether you meant anything by that."

"Something's happened between them, hasn't it?"

"It's nothing. I mean, I'm sure it's nothing."

JP hesitated, watching Alex carefully. He tossed up whether he should just give her a flat denial about seeing anything suspicious between Simon and Monique but her face was twisted with anxious uncertainty. He couldn't mislead her.

"Simon and Monique got out of the cab but instead of going straight inside they talked for quite a while; five minutes or so. I didn't know it was Simon at that stage but I have to say that from their body language I assumed he and Monique were a couple."

"What do you mean?"

"How do you explain the signals people give off? If you're asking me did they touch one another at all, then the answer is 'no'."

"Why didn't you tell me this before?" Alex snapped, battling to keep her voice from escalating into something that was loud and edgy.

"Because you're no fool, Alex. I knew that if there was something going on between Monique and Simon you'd work it out for yourself. And I didn't want you thinking I was trying to undermine your relationship with him because of the way I feel about you."

"Well, thanks very much for your support," she answered peevishly.

JP laughed in disbelief. "Don't attack me. I'm not one of your gossipy girlfriends."

"I just think you could have told me."

"When I got into your parents' house and saw the way he looked at you I discounted what I thought I'd seen but obviously you've found out there's something's between them. What's happened?"

But Alex wasn't able to reply because a whistling Mark Jackson suddenly bowled through the door laden with glasses, mineral water, potato chips and a topped up bottle of scotch, ready to move on to page thirty-six of his statement.

Hours later dinner was brought to the table for them all but it didn't improve the client's mental faculties. Finally, at close to eleven, JP sat back in his chair and announced he could do no more that evening. Mark Jackson swore in slurred speech and then announced he was going to buy both his guests a drink at the bar downstairs. He would not take 'no' for an answer.

JP looked across at Alex to gauge her reaction to Mark's unappealing offer. She shrugged indifferently; he suspected she was too exhausted to resist.

Minutes later the three of them were watching a handful of couples moving around a dance floor as an immaculately turned out gentleman played note perfect torch music on a grand piano. Mark Jackson swayed at the bar as he ordered a champagne cocktail for Alex, a beer for JP and another Scotch for himself.

But at that point JP remembered he'd made no arrangements to remove Mark's documents into safe storage overnight. He excused himself and wandered out into reception to discuss it with the night staff and as he hadn't been gone more than two minutes he was staggered to see Alex dancing with Mark on the dance floor when he returned.

He shook his head in disbelief that she would have agreed to it before noticing that she was in fact struggling to escape Mark's hold. She was no match for him. He had her well and truly pinned against his body, his hand slipping down and over her bottom where it parked itself.

With anger roaring up inside him he reached Mark and Alex in a few strides. Taking Mark's arm in a vice-like grip, he removed it from around Alex's waist.

"Sorry old man," JP explained. "We have a strict rule at the firm—no fraternising with the clients. I'm going to have to take over."

Mark Jackson's blood shot eyes had a dangerous glint to them. "Alex doesn't want to dance with you McKenzie. You ask her."

"Well actually Mark I did promise I'd have one dance with JP," she explained quickly, sinking with relief into JP's arms and allowing him to move her away to the other side of the dance floor. Behind them Mark tripped and stumbled his way back to the bar and JP suspected he'd spend the rest of the evening there until the hotel staff threw him out.

"Thank you," she said quietly to him. "I was scared to death. He literally dragged me onto the dance floor and then began to grope me. God, it was hideous! Can we get out of here JP, please? He really creeps me out!"

JP glanced across at Mark Jackson. He'd taken up his pew again at the bar but was watching the two of them dance with a dark and violent expression. "Let's just have this one dance as you said. If we leave now it might provoke him. He has a filthy temper when he's drunk and I'd rather not have a scene." JP smiled at her then. "By the way, I hope you realise that you just passed up an opportunity to join Mark's harem of current mistresses? He's been eyeing you off all day you know."

"Tempting," Alex laughed, edginess from her close encounter with Mark still rippling through her voice as she looked up at him to reveal dark shadows of exhaustion encircling her eyes, "And although I could have stood the drinking, the swearing and the ogling, I'd have had to draw the line at the burping."

JP gave a short laugh and gathered her closer; she was heaven in his arms.

"You did a great job today, Alex."

"Me? What about you? Mark was so difficult to pin down that I thought your head would explode at one point, but you kept at it anyway."

"Was that the point where he gave me five completely different versions of the one conversation?"

Alex nodded. "When you threw the pen down onto the table and shouted that if he didn't stop lying through his teeth you'd leave and wouldn't come back." Alex paused thoughtfully before going on. "Do you think you got the truth out of him in the end?"

"I got a version of the truth," JP conceded. "The problem with men like Mark Jackson is they think they're smarter than everyone else. What he doesn't realise is that in cross-examination a good Senior Counsel will unravel his lies so fast his head will be spinning and the next day they'll be all through the newspapers. All I can do is try and weed them out now before he gets into the witness box and perjures himself."

"I could never manage a client like you did today."

"Rubbish, it's just experience and confidence. One day you'll have both in spades."

His arms circled her waist then, her arms looping over and around his shoulders. They'd drawn so close it was hard to tell where one stopped and the other began. And despite all his promises, all his resolve, his body was raging with a fierce, sweet need to be one with her before the night was out.

He dropped his head a little so that his rough, unshaven cheek was tickled by the softness of her dark hair tumbling down around her face. "What happened during the break this afternoon?" he asked in her ear before pulling back a little so that he could watch her closely. "I want you to tell me Alex. Now. No arguments."

She watched him back, clearly too exhausted to fight his will that night, and in the next moment she was relating her conversation with Monique.

"There could be a perfectly innocent explanation," he offered when she'd finished but he couldn't hide the doubt in his voice.

"There could be but I don't think so." Alex's answer was despondent.

"Considering the skyrocket attraction between us you can hardly sit in judgment."

Suddenly her eyes were flashing their own skyrockets. "There's no comparison!" she snapped.

JP guffawed in bitter response. "I think if Simon had seen us together in my car the other night, or could even see us now, he'd disagree."

"Nothing happened between you and me that night and nothing's happening now."

"Whatever, but the real problem is you don't love Simon and you know that's the truth, you're just too terrified to admit it's over. But Simon knows it's over and he's beginning to make alternative plans for his future—a fallback position."

"You don't know that," Alex hurled at him.

"Trust me. I'm a man. I know what train of thought Simon's on. But if I were you I wouldn't beat myself up over it. In fact Alex, I'd like to see you cut loose for a while—from your parents, your fiancé, me, everyone. Then maybe you'll work out what you want and start fighting for it rather than drifting along with what everyone else in your life wants for you."

Alex stiffened in his arms like a board. "You know, if I'd wanted a lecture I'd have telephoned my mother!" With that she wriggled out of his hold, marched across the dance floor, snatched up her handbag from the bar and disappeared out the nearest exit.

JP thrust his hands deep into his pockets and followed in her wake, wandering slowly through reception and out through the hotel's front doors. He scanned the streetscape but there was absolutely no sign of her.

Shrugging his shoulders he swung on his heel and began to stroll towards his city apartment for a shower and a shave. One thing was for sure though, he wasn't about to slip into his pajamas and crawl into bed all alone that night. If Alex Farrer thought their conversation was over for the evening then she could think again.

When Alex burst through her front door she knew with absolute certainty that if she shut herself up inside her tiny apartment that night she would surely go mad. There was only one thing for it: water.

Within minutes she was diving into the deep end of her apartment complex's pool and cruising up and down its length with long, invigorating strokes. She reached fifty before she gave up counting the laps but she didn't let up on speed, not until she'd felt the familiar soothing ache in every one of her muscles; not until she was simply too exhausted to feel anything other than pure physical pain.

Only then, with murderous feelings towards JP beginning to subside, did Alex prop her arms on the edge of the pool and stop. Resting her cheek on the cool wet skin of her forearm she listened to melodic guitar music drifting from one of the apartments nearby. It rippled through the night air in time with the ripples still playing at the edges of the pool after her laps.

Ever since she'd been a little girl water had been her best friend; it hadn't let her down that night either. As always it soothed, comforted and inspired. Becoming a part of it had always helped her to see life with a frightening clarity. The only problem was that the clarity kicking in that night was whenever she thought about Simon.

She *did* want to marry Simon. Didn't she?

Before Alex could answer her own question she threw herself backwards and began a slow languorous backstroke up the pool. Only more swimming might shake off the doubts she was battling. But it was no use—even twenty more laps couldn't help her see a way forward that night. JP had addled her brain so completely that no amount of swimming was going to diffuse the endless questions swamping her: Did Simon love her? Did she love him? Would she make him happy?

Alex stopped in the middle of the pool, the water lapping around her shoulders like the doubts lapping at her mind and keeping time with the heavy, portentous pounding of her heart.

Would she make Simon happy?

She reached unsuccessfully for answers in the still, inky blackness of the warm night before diving down and swimming submerged to the far wall. By the time she'd burst to the surface for air she'd made her decision.

Enough was enough.

There would be no more JP and no more mind games. She would ring Simon that very night and make things right between them, once and for all.

Chapter Nine

Alex first saw him as she wandered up the dark garden pathway towards her apartment. He was leaning back against one of the stone pillars, a foot propped back against it, his arms folded across his chest, his expression pensive.

Alex stopped dead in her tracks, her eyes trailing compulsively over the powerful thighs in his jeans and the broad shoulders filling out the grey t-shirt clinging to his upper body like a second skin. His hair was damp from a recent shower, swept back from his forehead which was unconsciously lined with worry.

JP McKenzie.

Alex swallowed as an overwhelmingly urgent need to touch him and be touched by him banished the promise she'd made less than a quarter of an hour ago to exclude him from her heart and her mind once and for all.

She shivered then and moved forward to approach him and his attention was caught. He stood up straight, arms still folded, taking in the damp hair strewn about her shoulders and the surf towel knotted about her waist.

"What are you doing here?" she snapped nervously, praying he wouldn't notice the desire rising like a fine mist from her bare skin.

"I was worried about you." He strolled towards her and stopped very close, breaking every unspoken social law of personal space. "You rushed out of the hotel tonight and I wanted to make sure you got home okay. Your phone's switched off."

"Well as you can see I'm fine," she blurted, her pounding heart creating staccato notes of her words.

"Are you?" His voice was mellifluous and mellow, like golden syrup pouring over her skin. "You don't look it. In fact," he continued, taking yet another forbidden step into her personal space, "You've been like an emotional train wreck for most of the day."

Meanwhile Alex was screaming silently at herself to move: sideways, backwards—anywhere to put space between them so that she could collect her resolve and get inside to make that phone call to Simon. But she was frozen in time and space as JP filled her vision, her hearing, her sense of smell. All that was missing was taste and touch and that seductive notion made her bite her bottom lip in uneasy response.

"The only person turning me into an emotional train wreck is you," she replied but immediately regretted her words. JP would not let them go without comment and his mouth was already shifting into a satisfied smirk.

"An interesting admission," he purred finally, the edges of his eyes crinkling in that heart-stopping way of his.

172

"Not one you need to take any credit for," she argued, her chin rising so that she could look him clear in the eye.

"Oh really?"

"For some reason you've decided turning my life upside down should be taken on as a personal crusade," she began, seriously unnerved by his closeness. She was also trying to ignore the fact that his eyes were shamelessly resting on her lips, already full and sensitive. "You seem to have a problem with not trying to rescue me and I seem to have a problem with ... well, I have too many problems to list. But whatever is happening between us..."

"Falling in love?" JP's cobalt blue eyes were suddenly looking about as warm and inviting as the North Sea in winter.

"Don't," Alex snapped and with fingers chilled from her recent swim she fumbled uselessly to get her key into the door before the whole bunch fell with a clatter at JP's feet. He scooped them up immediately.

"Please can I have my keys," Alex demanded hotly.

JP turned to push the key into the door but instead of standing back and letting her in he pushed it open and stepped inside, holding it back for her to pass through into the hallway.

Alex gaped at him. "I'm not going in there with you," she objected, her heart racing at the prospect of being alone with him in her apartment. It was one thing to revolve around him in the confines of their busy office, quite another to spend time with him in her quiet, warm home with its soft lighting and romantic ambience.

"Yes, you are coming in," he demanded. "We have to talk and if we stay out here we'll have neighbours on our backs."

"I can't."

"Why not?"

"Because I don't trust you."

"You mean you don't trust yourself."

He raised questioning eyebrows at her when she didn't respond. And he was right. She didn't trust herself around him at all.

"There's been a significant development at work, Alex. I need you to know about it before you go back tomorrow." There was no teasing spark in his eyes now. His mouth was a straight, hard line.

"What is it?"

"Come inside. I'm not going to discuss it out here." He cocked his head in that way he did when he wanted her to follow him somewhere and then her legs were obeying and carrying her inside without reference to any direction from her head.

"What on earth is so important that it can't wait until tomorrow?" Alex asked when she'd moved into the dim hallway. She didn't like the fact that the two of them were sharing such a quiet, confined space but it was preferable to taking him any further into the intimate privacy of her small home.

"There'll be a new partner in the litigation section tomorrow."

"That's the news that couldn't wait?"

"Her name's Caroline Cartwright," he continued in a flat voice as though she hadn't spoken, as though he was willing himself to continue despite anything she might say.

Caroline, Alex thought to herself. Why was that name ringing a bell? Then it came back to her. Of course, the woman in the boutique and Marie from the legal centre had both asked after a 'Caroline' in his life.

"Until recently Caroline and I were in a serious two year relationship."

Alex searched his face for some indication of what he was feeling but it was a still mask in the grey light, the picture of control and neutrality. She just wished she could say the same about herself but she couldn't, for at that moment she was feeling very strange indeed.

The problem was she'd never, ever thought about JP in terms of anything but what he was to her. From day one he'd made her feel as though she was indispensably central to his life and yet it was a completely stupid and naïve notion. The truth was she'd never been anything to him but his PA: not his girlfriend, his wife, his lover, not even his friend.

"Are you okay, Alex?" He was looking at her very closely. She averted her look from his to avoid revealing the disquiet rumbling away inside her.

"Recently," Alex echoed hopelessly, hating herself for the effect his news was having upon her. She was engaged to Simon and this man was her boss. How could his personal life mean anything to her?

"Strictly between you and me, the original plan was that Caroline was going to head up litigation here. I was to stay in the UK and run the London office. Somehow we were going to try and maintain a long distance relationship. The fact that we believed we could do that probably didn't bode well for the long term. Anyway, we split up a few months ago and she decided to stay in London after all so I offered to come here to get litigation on its feet. It suited me anyway because I wanted an opportunity to work with Justin and Adam."

"I see," Alex whispered, nodding distractedly. "How long is Caroline staying?"

But what she didn't ask and what she really wanted to know was whether he was about to disappear back to London and out of her life as suddenly as he'd blown into it?

"I haven't spoken to her but I'm told she wants to join the office here permanently. She's arriving tomorrow to discuss it with my partners and me. I had no idea she would do this, Alex. Not even the other partners knew until she phoned Justin this morning. But what I really need you to know is that my relationship with her is over, no matter what you might think to the contrary."

"You don't have to explain anything to me."

"Of course I have to explain," he replied, exasperation sharpening his tone. "There's something happening between us Alex and denying it won't make it go away."

"Oh God, stop it!" Alex blocked her ears with her hands, her heart beating wildly as the tension mounted painfully at her temples. "You've let me know about Caroline and I appreciate it. But could you please leave now? You shouldn't be standing here in my hallway like this with all the lights off."

JP eyed her thoughtfully as he slipped a hand deep into one of his pockets. But then he shifted his stance and was reaching out for the door handle.

Alex could hardly breathe as she watched him. He was going to leave her, just as she'd asked. Within seconds she would be alone again, safe from the abyss of desire and temptation he'd been leading her inexorably towards. But then his hand stilled on the door handle, his eyes dark and fathomless, the hard angles of his jawline more rigid than ever. He leaned towards her a little and instinctively she drew back against the wall.

"First you have to tell me you don't want me to stay."

"I don't want you to stay," she whispered, her voice rasping as she basked in the heat of the desire burning white-hot in his eyes.

"Liar," he declared. "Tell me you don't want me to touch you."

"No, I don't want you to," she replied, shaking her head quickly but then a gasp broke free from her lips as his warm hands slid around the cool skin at her waist. His eyes lowered then as he shamelessly drank in the curves of her figure, looking at her near-naked body in a way no man had ever looked at her before.

Her eyelids dropped shut as she desperately tried to shut JP out so that she could remember who she was, what her responsibilities were, and then act decisively to counter the path he was leading her down. But closing her eyes only deepened her confusion as fingertips drifted away from her waist to trace a sensual, suggestive trail backwards and forwards, just above her bikini line.

"JP, you really need to leave now," she whispered and opened her eyes but it was too late. His other hand was now sliding decisively around her waist; he had no intention of going anywhere.

"I made a decision earlier tonight, Alex," he whispered with a slow shake of his head. "I'm not backing off from this anymore because we belong together and you know it."

Alex shook her head in anxious denial but his body pressed closer to hers, now shaking uncontrollably. She watched his hard, poised mouth, willing it to meet hers as she swallowed, her lips parting involuntarily as his thumb trailed across their shape in a gentle, yet proprietary gesture.

"You've completely done my head in, you know that don't you?" he murmured, his voice hoarse and unrecognizable as his other hand slid up her bare back and underneath her bikini strap, a look of deep satisfaction shining in his eyes as he watched her helpless quiver at his touch.

"We can't do this, JP! I don't want this."

"Perhaps you want this then."

His mouth brushed against hers very lightly before he drew away to watch her reaction. And evidently satisfied with what he saw he caught and released her mouth again, and then over and over, tantalising her without pity.

And right then Alex knew that JP knew she'd never, ever been kissed like that before; not with such provocative ease, tempting her further and further into a black hole of sweet, heady need for what he could make her feel that night, if she would only give in to what was happening between them, once and for all.

But she wouldn't do that. Her mind reached out to Simon and their years of commitment that had nothing to do with the tempest of feeling and sensation engulfing her that night. But JP was watching her with such fierce intensity again she couldn't hold a thought for more than a split second; each one was drifting away as quickly as it had arrived as she watched an unrelenting and hypnotic pinprick of light emerge from his dark eyes.

Finally his gaze dropped, moving remorselessly across her figure before his hands lifted to cradle her face, tilting it purposefully towards his. And with a barely audible groan his mouth seized hers, demanding that her own yield and succumb to his immediately. In the next moment their mouths were searching each other's and in mindless, disembodied response Alex heard a moan rise up from deep within herself as she responded with uncontained fervour. On and on it went, an exquisite journey of discovery as their tongues met and he sighed helplessly into her mouth as Alex revelled in the power she knew she held over him.

But she was equally lost within his power too, for heat was raging in waves across her skin, plummeting like a fireball of need and desire into her lower stomach and thighs as his hips pinned her against the wall and shifted restlessly against hers. And with their mouths clinging together, his hands buried themselves in her hair as hers crept stealthily beneath his shirt to explore the depression below his broad chest muscles and the ridges of his flat, hard stomach. In the next moment she'd found the button and zipper of his jeans and was unfastening them as swiftly and decisively as if she had unfastened them a hundred times before.

And it was then Alex knew JP had found a woman within her she'd never known existed before. A woman she feared and yet understood. A woman he knew was his soul mate.

JP tore his lips from hers and cradled her head in his hands.

"Wait, Alex," JP panted, his chest heaving with tormented desire. "I don't want to go on with this unless you can tell me it's over with him once and for all."

But then they both jumped violently. Alex's home phone was ringing out into the night like a jarring peal of accusation. They stared at each other as mutual acknowledgement seeped through their expressions: Simon.

"Don't answer it!" JP's hips pinned her against the wall with fresh purpose.

Alex squirmed uselessly to be free of his weight. "Please, let me go," she begged. "It's Simon. If I don't answer he'll know something is wrong between us. I can't do that to him."

"Something is wrong," JP snarled. "You're in love with me, Alex, not him. Choose between us—now."

Was she being ripped in two? God help her but it felt like that. On the other end of the phone was a man who for years had loved the compliant, perfect Alex she'd offered up to him and the world. But in her arms was the man who saw her just as she was, complex and so very imperfect, yet he wanted her body and soul. It was then she knew that her choice was not about JP or Simon, it was about choosing herself—once and for all.

"Let me go, JP!" she cried out, unable to shift his weight and becoming frenzied as she realised Simon would not wait on much longer.

JP withdrew his arms from around her waist and stepped back. Alex rushed to the phone as it rang out and reached for the receiver. But her fingertips paused on top of it as she was struck down by indecision.

Her eyes swept in panic to JP who was standing just metres from her, his face set with grim, obdurate lines as he fastened his jeans, slowly and deliberately. They were frozen in time, the phone ringing out as his gaze searched hers savagely. Then he muttered words which she knew would chill her to the bone for as long as she lived: "If you answer that phone it's over for us, and I won't be back."

But Alex's hand had already closed around the receiver and was lifting it slowly to her ear.

Chapter Ten

The day was already heating up like a pressure cooker even though it was barely eight-thirty in the morning. Making things worse was the oppressively hot westerly wind howling up Bridge Street as Alex wandered towards her office building, exhaustion settling like lead weight into every muscle of her body. For after her torrid half-hour phone call with Simon the night before she'd had no sleep at all.

Tossing and turning all night her mind had played back the endless round of blurted apologies and explanations. Yet by the end of the phone call nothing had been resolved between them except the most serious thing of all: their long relationship was coming to an end.

They'd decided to meet in the foyer of her building after work that day so that they could go somewhere private and talk things through. But Alex knew there was no turning back.

Simon was devoted and decent but he would never be the man for her. And she would never be the woman for him. He'd fallen in love with a dream girl and for three long years she'd let him live the dream. She would never forgive herself for doing that to him because now the dream was lifting like a summer morning's mist. But she couldn't pretend for a minute longer that she was anything more than who she was:

an ordinary girl, falling in love for the first time, longing to stop dreaming and start living—the ordinary girl JP had noticed when she was still well hidden under layers of muddy, bedraggled clothing.

Alex hesitated outside the building. Simon's misery weighed heavily upon her spirits and she felt totally ill equipped to walk into an office dominated by JP's phone calls, clients and staff. As always he would be like an omnipotent, inescapable presence within and it took every ounce of her willpower to step into the foyer's perpetually revolving doors.

When minutes later she walked out of the lift at level twenty-three the last person she expected to see was waiting for her in reception. Her father sat perched on the edge of a chair looking small and uneasy amidst the elaborate décor of Griffen Murphy Lawyers.

Alex was dumbfounded.

Her parents never visited her at work, not even when they were visiting the city. She'd sometimes wondered whether they might be intimidated by the severe, corporate surroundings of her law firm. For even though her father had run a successful building business for forty years, he and Mary avoided busy, crowded places now, preferring a quiet life at home surrounded by their family.

Peter Farrer struggled onto his wobbly knees when he saw Alex walking towards him. Holding out his arms he pulled her close.

"This is a nice surprise," Alex smiled down at her diminutive father. "Where's Mum?" They were rarely apart.

"She's at the dentist, poor love. I can't stay too long."

"Is she okay?"

"Yes, yes. Just a routine check-up."

"Oh okay, that's good," Alex nodded, still wondering why he'd made the effort to come in to see her. "Would you like a cup of coffee?"

"No I'm fine. I've just had one." Peter Farrer was looking around himself anxiously.

Alex bit down on her bottom lip. Something was bothering her father and she was about to ask him what it was when the lift doors opened and JP McKenzie sauntered into reception rolling an enormous trolley of folders behind him.

Alex froze, helplessly railing at herself to reel in her gaze as she drank in the sight of him, so incredibly gorgeous in his navy suit and open necked white shirt—how could she ever have thought his looks ordinary?

JP noticed Alex and an unreadable expression crossed his face. There was a hesitation in his gait momentarily but he then changed direction to move towards her and her father. At that point Peter Farrer saw him too and Alex noticed the delighted smile that spread across her father's face.

JP held out his hand and shook Peter's warmly, keeping his look well averted from Alex's. It was a stab in the heart but she knew JP would be true to his word of the night before: she was history and he didn't care if she knew it.

"Are you going to charge me for that handshake?" Peter Farrer asked, his eyes shining teasingly.

"Aye, but don't worry. Family of staff are entitled to a discount," JP quipped back quickly, his mouth playing with a smirk before adding, "Four hundred an hour for you."

"Oh no!" Alex's father responded, laughing brightly.

"I didn't think you'd be back until lunchtime," Alex broke in, her voice barely concealing its nervous tremor.

JP turned towards her slowly as though reluctant to expend the effort on the movement, his cutting look finally slashing a swathe of agony through her insides. "I saw the client again early this morning. I can do the rest from here. How's Mrs Farrer?" JP turned back to Alex's father.

"She's well. She would have liked to have seen Alex too but she's in the dentist's chair."

"Why don't you bring her here afterwards? Have you seen where Alex works, through those doors?"

"No we haven't but we'd better not today. We have a train to catch."

"Maybe some other time then."

"That would be terrific," Peter replied before changing tack and asking whether JP had seen the soccer on the TV late the night before, a mutual passion they'd discovered when JP had been at his home.

JP flashed the briefest of blue-eyed looks at Alex who could feel the blush spreading up her neck, through her cheeks and into the roots of her hair. "Ah ... no," he began hesitantly. "It wasn't on until after midnight and I was ... fully occupied at that time."

"You missed a great game. A great game." Peter Farrer effused.

JP and Peter chatted for a few minutes about the respective strengths and weaknesses of various football teams. Meanwhile, Alex began to fidget and glance around; JP had an office to run and yet he seemed completely comfortable about whiling away his time with his PA's father so that he could discuss football!

"Hang on, I've just remembered something," JP declared and reached into his suit jacket for his wallet. After fishing around within it he took out two tickets of some kind and thrust them into Peter Farrer's hand.

"What are these?"

"They're for the A-league match at the stadium on Saturday night," JP explained.

"I can't accept them,," Peter protested. "That's far too generous."

Alex could tell her father was bowled over by the gesture.

"Of course you can take them," JP insisted. "They're corporate box seats so you'll have a great view. Do you know anyone who'd like the second ticket?"

"Of course, but I can't..."

"Peter, take them. Please. I'd like you to have them."

Alex watched as her father gave JP a short, sharp male nod conveying all the gratitude and delight he was feeling. But then JP was excusing himself and without looking at Alex again he disappeared through the door behind them to the back offices beyond reception.

"At the ripe old age of seventy I may have to take back all the things I've said about lawyers." Peter Farrer then turned to Alex and added, "Particularly if my daughter is going to be one."

Alex looked long and hard at her father. Was this why he'd arrived in her office that morning—to let her know she had his support?

"Nothing's settled yet, Dad. It may not happen."

"Well that's all right, too," he replied simply. "So long as you know you have your mother and me behind you, no matter what you decide ... and that goes for any part of your life."

"Thank you," Alex whispered croakily, guessing he was referring to more than just her career choices.

"Your mother told me you're unhappy. She said you feel we've pushed you into certain things," Peter explained uncertainly. He wasn't adept at heart to hearts, particularly with his daughter.

"I was unfair to Mum on the phone yesterday," Alex confessed as she wiped away tears that had sprung up from nowhere. "It isn't her fault. None of this is her fault, or yours. You and Mum..."

"Alexandra, let me say my bit," Peter interrupted. "I've been thinking and your mother and I have been talking. The thing is, you may be right. You're a good girl. You're mother and I are so proud. We just want the best for you. You were our miracle baby when we'd long given up any hope of children and so you became the centre of our universe. And I know we're elderly and old fashioned. We don't really understand the world you move in and to be honest, I think we've been too hard on you—pushing you in certain directions. Do you understand what I'm trying to say?"

Alex nodded, overwhelmed at the enormity of the admission from her proud, single-minded father.

"You need to make up your own mind about who and what's best for you. We know you'll make the right choice and we'll be there whatever you decide. That's all I wanted to say."

"You know already, don't you Dad. You know there's not going to be a wedding with Simon. It's over—as of last night.

Peter Farrer nodded quickly. "You're mother and I guessed that would happen and that's okay. As I said, we just want you to be happy and we're there for you—always."

Alex wrapped her arms around her father and clung onto him as he hugged her back. But then he was shuffling off to the lift. He had said what he wanted to say from the bottom of his heart and with great love but he would linger no longer, uncomfortable with emotional displays.

Lost in troubled thoughts Alex turned and wandered through the door to the offices behind reception, and even in her distraction noticed straight away that most of the workstations were empty. She wondered where everyone was and then she heard JP's voice; it could be very loud at times. He was leading a robust discussion in the conference room. Picking up the odd word here and there Alex guessed the topic was rugby. Plans were being made and strategies laid down for the match the following day: litigation versus commercial or in other words, JP McKenzie versus Justin Murphy. Without hesitation she walked as quickly as possible past the open conference room door. She was in no mood for office rugby matches or another run in with JP.

"Alex! I need you in here!" JP shouted above the general din. She stopped dead in her tracks before turning around and walking reluctantly into the room, cursing the radar he threw out whenever she was around.

Lawyers and PAs were gathered. There was a lot of laughing, finger pointing, wise cracks and shouting about who should or shouldn't be on the team for the match against the commercial section of the firm. JP had a notebook in his hand and was leaning on the lectern in one corner of the room. As she entered he looked across at her with little acknowledgement.

"Okay. Alex is here so we're up to nine," he shouted over the light-hearted cacophony of noise.

"Who wants girls' germs on the team? Not me!" Michael Porter, one of the junior lawyers shouted as he winked at Alex teasingly.

"Now listen," JP announced with mock impatience, a wry smile on his lips. "Commercial think they've got all the endurance and that litigators are just a bunch of mangy, twenty-second sprinters. I know Alex can swim fifty lengths of a swimming pool without missing a beat so I'll have at least one staff member who won't keel over with a heart attack—unlike most of you blokes." With that there was an onslaught of boos and cheers.

"Do I have any say in this?" Alex asked, just loud enough to be heard by JP over the racket. Lifting his eyebrows he gave her a stern, slow shake of the head.

Alex nodded blankly as if to say 'I thought so', and turning on her heel walked out of the room.

It was useless to argue.

When JP wanted something, nothing and nobody could stop him. He'd decided to make her play rugby the next day, despite what had happened between them the night before and despite the fact he would guess that rugby was out of her comfort zone. But knowing JP that was precisely why he was making her do it.

"So you're still here!" Vera Boyd drawled with a humourless smile that clashed with the snakiness in her voice.

"Still where?" Alex shot back in irritation.

She knew she shouldn't have gone in search of Vera, but she'd returned from lunch to find JP had disappeared from the office after his rugby recruitment drive leaving only a few jobs for her, one of which involved lengthy and convoluted amendments to Mark Jackson's statement. She'd completed those and unable to bear sitting around and thinking about the events overtaking her personal life, had resolved to ask Vera if she needed help with anything, despite her better instincts.

"Still in Jonathan McKenzie's office?"

"Clearly." Alex was too tired to conceal the sarcasm in her tone.

"Well, I hope you enjoy it then," Vera tossed at her in a bored fashion. Only then did Alex notice that all the threat had left Vera's voice since they had last spoken. She wondered whether she should be worried about that.

"You'll have your time cut out then. I don't envy you. I can't understand a thing that man says or does."

"What are you talking about?"

"Haven't you noticed he speaks in riddles?"

"Not really. His instructions are brief but usually pretty clear."

"And as for his handwriting, I can't read a word of it. He's quite impossible to work for generally, you know. He shouts out of his office when he wants something. He gets impatient if you don't understand what he's talking about instantly. He wants me to change everything David Griffen and I set up. I just can't work for someone like that," she finished primly.

"What are you saying, Vera?" Alex's pulse was racing as once again her future seemed to be hanging in the balance. "Are you moving away from JP's office?"

Vera gawked at Alex as if she was the stupidest person she'd ever met. "Don't you know yet? Jonathan called me this morning. He said that in light of my expertise as a high-level PA he wanted me to work for Caroline Cartwright and settle her in."

Alex gaped at Vera dumbstruck.

"There's no need to look like that, Alex," Vera went on superciliously. "You should be grateful your job with Jonathan is secure." With that she turned back to her computer screen, giving Alex the clear signal that the conversation was over.

Alex wandered back towards her desk in a stupor.

What on earth was JP's game plan?

Wouldn't he have leapt upon a PA reshuffle opportunity to get her out of his office after his ultimatum of the night before? Yet moving Vera sideways to Caroline's office and making her his sole PA didn't seem consistent with that. She ran her hands through her hair in confusion, unable to make out what was going on at all.

Hearing JP's voice in his office she picked up Mark Jackson's amended affidavit and wandered in. Her eyes were lowered to the document, double-checking the formal parts on the front page, as she approached his desk.

"I thought you might want this back straight away..." she began as she looked up from the page in front of her but then stopped dead.

Perching on the side of JP's desk was without a doubt the most stunningly beautiful woman Alex had ever seen in the flesh, and somehow she knew instinctively that it had to be Caroline Cartwright.

She had the peaches and cream skin that only women of the highest northern latitudes could retain. Her hair was platinum in colour and hung like silk to her shoulders. She was tall and slender in her fitted silver-blue suit and she looked across at Alex with opaque grey eyes, regarding her with the quiet composure of a cat.

JP was standing very close to her; the two of them had been talking in hushed tones. Alex was mortified she'd disturbed their private moment.

"I'm sorry," she gushed, feeling herself turn pink. "I didn't know ... I didn't realise..." But she couldn't finish her sentence. She had to take a deep breath to steady herself before she lost her cool completely.

JP straightened. Both he and Caroline were staring at her and Alex had never felt more self-conscious in her life.

"Alex, I'd like you to meet Caroline Cartwright. Alex is my PA—for the time being," he added gratuitously, his expression remaining stony and distant.

"Hello," Alex responded.

"Hello, Alex," Caroline replied pleasantly.

She had the voice of a woman who'd been raised with every privilege life could offer. It was lilting, with a musical, unhurried cadence and Alex suspected it had commanded the attention of prime ministers and royalty alike.

"It's Mark Jackson's affidavit," Alex explained, approaching JP just close enough to reach out and hand him the document. It was quivering a little with the tremble in her hand and he flashed a knowing look at her as he took it.

"Thank you," he acknowledged quietly, searching her face before she turned and rushed towards the door. But Caroline Cartwright's tinkly, amused comment reached Alex's ears before she was barely through it, "Funny little mouse!"

With that Alex covered her mouth and ran towards the ladies bathroom. She thought she might be torn apart by the burgeoning ache in her chest as she finally burst into a cubicle, locked the door and lowered herself onto the closed toilet lid, fighting for breath.

Oh God, to have a woman like Caroline hand down such a contemptuous judgment of her, and in front of JP too. A funny little mouse: Alex had never been so humiliated in all her life.

And burying her face in her hands she promptly burst into tears, the unbearable pain lashing her like countless whip strokes that she couldn't escape, no matter how much she twisted and turned.

All day her insides had been coiling up into a taut spool of unhappiness, self-blame and despair. And now her life was crashing down around her.

Simon was gone, devastated by her sudden demolition of their long relationship. Her parents too, deeply hurt by her professed unhappiness, had set her free and withdrawn. Next it would be JP who would vanish from her life—just as he'd promised the night before.

She'd finally found the freedom to be who she wanted to be, only to discover that she was about to end up lonelier and unhappier than she'd ever thought possible. She hardly knew herself, cut loose as JP had said from everything that had anchored and defined her until that point.

Fighting back deep, painful sobs Alex bit down on her knuckle to silence herself, swaying backwards and forwards in repetitive motion. Gradually, the searing agony of total emotional breakdown eased and an eerie quiet calm replaced the tumult. Little by little clear, rational convictions began to fill the vacuum that heartache had carved out within her.

For so long she'd been immersed in being someone's daughter, fiancée or employee she'd hardly ever thought of herself as someone with an independent existence. And yet there she was, sitting in the ladies' bathroom of all places, facing the life-changing revelation that the person she should have been looking to all along for the strength she needed to be herself, was herself.

Caroline's stinging belittlement had simply been the straw that had broken the camel's back. But Alex vowed she would never again rely on anyone else to distinguish her. She would rise or fall on her own merits and on her own terms. In every part of her life she would be true to herself.

She sighed resignedly then. But for JP her old life would not have splintered around her. He'd pushed and pushed until finally she was forced to see that everything she'd built around herself was a house of cards. She wished she could feel angry with him but she couldn't. She could only ever love him for seeing her for what she was and not accepting anything less from her. He believed in her, more profoundly than she'd ever believed in herself—until that moment.

And with that belief came the realisation that she had fallen in love with JP McKenzie.

She loved the way he could read her like a book. She loved that he laughed at her when she was getting far too serious. She loved the way he made her feel when he held her, when he looked at her with those incredible eyes. But most of all, she loved that she finally knew what it felt like to want to spend the rest of your life with one person.

But with a start Alex sensed that she was no longer alone in the bathroom. Someone had entered and was calling her name quietly.

It was Sophie.

Alex stood and opened the cubicle door before emerging to see her friend's anxious look.

"Alex, are you all right? Jonathan McKenzie came to me saying he thought you may be unwell and could I check if you were in the bathroom. Are you sick?"

"No, just exhausted."

"You look dreadful! Come on, it's right on five o'clock. Let's get out of here and we can go somewhere and talk."

Alex bit down on her lip and looked wildly at the ceiling to try and fight off the tears that threatened again. "I can't. I have to meet Simon."

"Can't you put him off tonight? You clearly need some girl therapy."

Alex shook her head in reply.

"Why not?" Sophie argued insistently. "What's so important that you need to meet Simon tonight?"

"We broke off our engagement over the phone last night. I'm meeting him one last time so that we can deal with it face to face."

Sophie stared at Alex in disbelief. "You're kidding," she whispered. Alex shook her head.

"What a nightmare," Sophie murmured in a state of shock as she rested her hands on Alex's shoulders. "No wonder you look like something out of the body snatchers."

"I need a favour," Alex asked, urgency in her voice.

"Anything," Sophie agreed nodding.

"I need you to go and tell Jonathan I'm not feeling well and that I'm going home. Tell him it's just a headache. Then I need you to find my handbag and bring it back here so that I can get across to the lift and meet Simon downstairs."

"Well I'll try but Jonathan was pretty insistent I bring you to his office. He's not going to be happy."

But Sophie did as she was asked and Alex was forced to wait what felt like endless minutes as she paced the ladies bathroom. When Sophie finally returned she looked triumphant.

"Mission accomplished!" she announced. "He was on the phone so I did the handbag thing first. I'll have to go straight back now to let him know you've gone home. Are you going to be all right?"

Alex nodded. "Thank you, Soph. I don't know what I'd do without you." The two girls clung onto one another before Alex squeezed her friend's hands, gave her a long reassuring look and then made her way quickly out of the bathroom and across to the lifts.

Once on the ground floor she found a quiet, well-concealed corner to stand in while she waited for Simon, and she was soon thanking her lucky stars she had because JP appeared out of nowhere.

With her pulse racing Alex watched him as he thrust his hands deep into his pockets and walked straight past her, across the foyer and out of the building. She could still catch glimpses of him through the revolving doors as he stood on the street outside and turned his head from side to side as though he was looking for someone, but for once his radar failed him.

He disappeared amidst the moving sea of pedestrians outside just before Simon wandered into the building. Unlike JP, Simon saw her immediately and with a haunted look he approached her and took her in his arms. Alex sunk into them, the temptation to regress back into their familiarity and safe harbour almost overwhelming. But she quickly prised herself away. She'd done enough damage in his life already and would not play with his feelings any longer.

"Where would you like to go?" he asked as they wandered out into the heat of the early evening and paused outside. Alex looked around nervously but thankfully JP had vanished.

"I don't mind. Anywhere where we can talk and have a drink,"

"Why don't we go down to the Frog and Toad ... look, isn't that your boss?"

Alex swung around in the direction Simon was facing. JP stood a short distance away with a hand on an open cab door as Caroline Cartwright slipped into the back seat ahead of him. He was motionless as he searched the crowded street. But his gaze bypassed Alex and Simon altogether and with that he turned and folded himself into the cab next to Caroline and slammed the door behind himself. And as he did so Alex watched on, mesmerised by the irrevocable finality of that moment, as JP's taxi pulled out into the bustle of the traffic and disappeared.

Chapter Eleven

The knocking went on and on. It merged with her dreams until finally its persistence roused Alex from the deepest of slumbers. She lay there motionless, unsure where she was and struggling to put together the pieces of her life in any kind of sensible order. But as she opened her eyes and looked around she realised she was in her own apartment. Morning light was filtering through the lush garden outside her window and casting a lime green hue throughout her bedroom.

With a groan she rolled over. The sleeping pill she'd taken the night before was drugging her every thought and movement. But with a dull ache pounding away inside her she started to piece together the night before with Simon and a renegade tear of emotional exhaustion rolled down her cheek.

The knocking began again and Alex eased herself up into a sitting position in her bed. Then she heard a voice at the door and it was with relief that she guessed it was Sophie.

"Alex, wake up now! I know you're in there!" she yelled.

With heavy legs and an addled head, Alex placed her feet gingerly on the floor and stumbling out to the front door opened it to find Sophie's expression tense and expectant.

"Last night you looked rung out with exhaustion. Now you look as though you've had an overdose of sleep."

"I took a sleeping pill," Alex explained, turning around and traipsing back inside to turn the coffee machine on. Sophie followed.

"How are you?" she asked tentatively. "How was last night?"

"Dreadful," Alex admitted wretchedly. "He was crying. I was crying. It was just appalling."

"How is he taking it?"

"Good and bad," Alex recounted bleakly. "He said he'd sensed something was coming, that I seemed unhappy, but he wasn't sure whether it was just the changes at work."

"Was he angry?"

Alex thought over Sophie's question, trying to make sense of her disheveled memories. "No, more resigned," she replied eventually. "He said he'd felt he'd been clinging on to me for some time, as though I was trying to escape. Imagine that Sophie, it must have been awful for him."

"I know it's hard to get your head around things this morning but he will get through this Al. He's an attractive guy and he'll meet someone who's better suited to him—it's just a matter of time."

"He has already," Alex admitted. She needed Sophie to know so that the news, when it eventually reached her friend's ears, would not be a shock. "He and Monique are going to start spending time together."

Sophie's hand rose to cover her mouth as she gaped at Alex. "Are you serious?" she asked finally and Alex nodded.

"When did that start?"

Alex turned away to steam up some milk.

"He told me it had been creeping up on both of them for awhile. Monique had made no secret of the fact she was crazy about him and I'd been making him feel unhappy and unwanted for ages."

"How do *you* feel about it though?"

"It feels strange but I know I'll be fine about it with time," she confessed, feeling a surge of relief on that point at least. "I know Monique will make him happier than I ever could."

"No regrets then?"

"About breaking off the engagement—none. About the way I treated him—plenty."

"Don't be too hard on yourself. You didn't plan for it to turn out like this."

"That doesn't change the fact that because of me Simon's wasted three years of his life."

"I'm sure he doesn't look at it that way."

"Then he should, because I am to blame for it," Alex declared.

"Alex, life's not a machine. It doesn't always go the way we want it to because sometimes other things take over. Speaking of which, you'll have to hurry up after that coffee and get dressed. That indomitable boss of yours has got a bee in his bonnet about this rugby match today and your name's on the list."

Alex groaned. She'd forgotten all about the match and wondered whether she would ever throw off the effects of the sleeping pill so that she could run around a sports field that morning.

"You'll have to be a saint to keep working for him you know," Sophie added thoughtfully as she sipped her freshly brewed coffee. "He's so grumpy sometimes. You should have heard him when I told him you'd left for the day yesterday ... oh, I had to tell him about you breaking up with Simon, I'm sorry."

"Don't worry about it," Alex reassured her, knowing he'd guess as much within about five minutes of seeing her—she could hide nothing from him.

"But then he can be very persuasive too when he wants to be," Sophie prattled on distractedly. "I told him you had a headache but he didn't accept it. He just kept firing questions at me until I heard myself telling him you were under a lot of pressure because you were calling off your engagement. Come to think of it, I don't remember how he managed to prise it out of me."

"He's a litigator. That's his job."

"I wouldn't like to be cross-examined by him if my reputation was on the line," Sophie mused out loud. "Anyway, he backed right off and was quite pleasant once he heard the reason you'd left. He seemed to accept that breaking off an engagement was a good excuse for a PA to flee from work."

"I guess I'll find out pretty soon whether or not he still feels that way," Alex replied dubiously.

But as Alex stood under her hot shower a short time later she began to wonder why, given the turmoil of the last few days, she was feeling a very new and very strange sense of lightness, as though someone had lifted a hundred kilos of weight from her shoulders. And despite her apprehension about facing JP that day the feeling of lightness was growing steadily with every passing minute. And only then did Alex understand what it was.

She wasn't worrying about disappointing anyone anymore.

She remembered that feeling of long ago when her life had been simple and anxiety free. But at some point over the last few years she'd taken on the enormous burden of trying to be too many things to too many people—no more.

Sophie was right. Simon would be okay; she knew that. The only person she had to make sure she didn't let down now was herself, and she was determined that would never happen.

JP had summed it up two nights before when he'd told her he wanted to see her fight for what she wanted. Well, from this day onwards she would do just that. She would seize her dreams and make them a reality, no matter how impossible the odds. In her own quiet way, she knew her life was going to be very different.

Now all she had to do was bottle that feeling and radiate it around herself. And she'd start that very morning with JP because she knew she wanted him to be a part of her life more than anything else in the world.

There was just one problem—a small chink in her new armour of optimism. Sure, she may have decided she wanted JP but that didn't mean he was there for the taking. After all, two nights ago they'd mutually banished one another from their personal lives for good. And yesterday he was disappearing in cabs to mystery destinations with his all too recent ex-girlfriend.

Well too bad. When she walked into that office today it would be as though she were meeting him again for the first time. She would hold her head high and be utterly professional. Being with JP on any level was the only thing that mattered, even if the only relationship he would offer her was as her boss, and probably only briefly at that.

Cathy, the firm receptionist, beamed at the two girls as they walked into Griffen Murphy Lawyers half an hour later.

"They've all gone!" she announced before the girls had time to speak. "Everyone from commercial and litigation has headed over to the rugby field already. You'll have to hurry up," she advised, calling out good luck as they disappeared back into the lift.

Less than ten minutes later, as she and Sophie made their way down through the Domain parkland beyond the Art Gallery of New South Wales, Alex could see a crowd had already gathered beside the rugby field. Small groups of staff from the firm were lazing about on the hill next to it and enjoying the warm, soon to be blistering, summer sun. However, there were two other groups kitted out in sports gear who were milling about next to the sidelines. Even from a distance Alex could tell they were swapping tactics and pep talks.

She saw JP almost immediately in the middle of one of the groups. He was wearing a footy singlet and shorts, and although not the tallest man in the litigation team his sheer size seemed to dwarf them all. He emanated power from the bulk of his shoulders, chest and arms, soon to be called into impenetrable rigidity when the game began. Alex remembered what his protective motives were for first developing that build and wished she could return to that night in his car when he'd shared them with her, especially now that she might never share an intimate moment like that with him again.

Alex approached the group. A couple of the team members stood back to let her join in and at that moment Michael Porter, often short on office etiquette, let out a long, cool wolf whistle for her benefit.

"It's okay!" Alex announced as she took up a position in the circle and rubbed her hands together before continuing with a grin, "You can all relax. Your star player has arrived."

She beamed at everyone and then drove her gaze at JP. He was already busy checking out her outfit: lightweight black shorts, singlet top and running shoes.

But JP sensed instantly there was something else that was different about Alex Farrer that morning. For a start, there was an easy confidence about her he'd never seen before. She was holding herself tall and upright and her eyes were shining as she took in everything going on around her. In fact, everyone was looking at her because she was simply compelling to watch.

"Exactly how many games of football have you played in your lifetime, Alex?" Michael Porter teased.

"Absolutely none!" she declared and smiled self-deprecatingly.

"But as the boss says," Michael continued with a cheeky grin. "Alex can swim like a fish so in the event of a tsunami across this rugby field we're set!"

"Okay, very funny. If you two have finished we'll get on with things," JP began, rubbing his hands together and bouncing up and down on the spot in a quick warm up that soon had a few of the others following suit. "Now as I was saying, commercial, after all their big talk, have arrived here today and are down two players. And outrageous as it is they've asked me to send one of my players over to even up the numbers."

"No way!" someone called out in mock protest.

"That's typical of commercial lawyers," Michael Porter shouted. "They're full of big talk, but when things don't go their way they go to water. They just can't hack the pressure like litigators can."

"You're exactly right Michael," JP agreed, egging on his team's competitive zeal. "But we can't have commercial saying we beat the pants off them because we were up a player. We need to beat the pants off them with equal numbers. So who's volunteering?"

He was met with a stony silence.

"Come on guys," he prodded. "Someone's got to do it."

"I'll go!" Alex offered. Everyone turned to her.

"No way, not Alex," Michael Porter protested with a shout.

"No, not you, Alex," JP agreed in swift confirmation and turned to the others.

"Why not?" she argued. Again, all faces turned back to her. "Look I know I'm your star player but you can't have them saying you sent over the weakest link, can you?" she finished jokingly.

With that, Alex turned on her heel and began to saunter over to the commercial group before anyone else could argue.

"Alex!" JP called out behind her, craving a moment of her exclusive attention before she disappeared across to the opposition. She turned and waited for him to catch up.

"Are you sure you don't mind? I dragged you into this game after all."

"I don't mind," she answered brightly and began to walk backwards, her ponytail swinging from side to side as she moved towards her new team. "Anyway," she tossed at him with a teasing, heart catching grin, crinkling her nose a little as she squinted into the bright morning sunshine. "It'll give me a chance to check out whether any of the commercial partners are looking for a new PA seeing as I'm only in that role with you—for the time being," she added, echoing his words to Caroline Cartwright of two days ago.

She threw him a cryptic smile before swinging around and continuing on, a tiny bounce in her walk. And her upbeat, positive mood didn't end there. She joined in with the sparring and the good-natured but ferocious competitiveness, the high-fives and the friendly abuse of poor David from the mailroom who'd foolishly volunteered to referee the game.

And despite her self-deprecatory remarks about her rugby prowess, once she had the ball she was surprisingly difficult to catch before she tore across the score line. At one stage Michael Porter even took to chasing and holding her in his arms whenever play started so that no one could pass the ball to her.

But in the end litigation won the day, although commercial wanted a right of challenge to follow in the next few weeks. Justin was insistent that Alex become commercial's official mascot, thereby banned from playing with litigation in the future. JP was equally insistent that she was on temporary loan and would definitely not be playing for commercial again. In fact, the pulsating imperative within him to keep Alex as close as possible on every level was escalating to a point where any other outcome was becoming unthinkable.

Chapter Twelve

When Alex walked into JP's office, freshly showered and back in her work clothes after their morning rugby match, she didn't have her head buried in any documents. It was held high.

He'd been dictating quietly but his words trailed off as he watched her approach his desk. He leant back in his office chair slowly and stretched his arms back to lock his hands behind his head, regarding her curiously.

"You have a message from Mark Jackson," she explained in a business like tone of voice.

"He rang *you?*"

"You were on the phone."

"What did he say?" JP beckoned to her with his finger to sit down opposite him.

"I wrote it down in short hand," Alex perched on the edge of one of his client chairs. "I thought I should take it down verbatim so that you had the precise meaning of his message. In the interests of decorum I've changed some wording which will become apparent to you."

"Okay," JP murmured slowly, wishing he knew where Alex was going with all her newfound professional formality. "Shoot."

"Here I go." Alex began to read in a monotone fashion. "Is that you, Alex? Good. At last they've put me through to someone I know in that den of thieves you work in. Your boss is on the line to someone else who he's no doubt robbing every last cent from, so pass this message on, will you? Tell Jonathan McKenzie from me that I got his letter. If he thinks I'm going to pay all my outstanding debts to your firm before he'll accept another matter from me then he can go and expletive himself. Then you can tell him I never said those things he's put into my expletive affidavit at paragraph forty and I don't care how many expletive documents he reckons he can find that prove I said them. And you can also tell him that if he doesn't expletive wake up to himself and let the client run the show instead of expletive banging on with legal mumbo jumbo all the time then he'll have no expletive clients left."

JP stared at Alex and then throwing his head back began to laugh helplessly. For the first time since entering his office, Alex smiled.

"So what did you say back to him?"

"I said I'd pass the message on."

"Ever the cool professional, eh Alex?"

"What will happen with Mark now?" Alex deftly ignored his sardonic remark.

"With any luck he'll do as he's threatened and find another lawyer. But I suspect what will actually happen is he'll sober up, pay his bills and as his lawyers we'll all move on for another five years of having to put up with him."

Alex nodded and was silent as their eyes locked but then she got to her feet and was taking steps backwards towards the door.

"Okay," she said lightly, "Well that's all. I'll let you get on with dictating now."

But JP wasn't having it. He got to his feet and with his longer stride reached the door before her and slammed it shut.

"Oh no you don't," he muttered, hearing an involuntary hint of menace in his tone. "You don't escape that easily. You've been avoiding me too long already."

"Why, do you have something else for me to do?" she asked, feigning wide-eyed innocence.

JP narrowed his eyes in response. "Aye, I do," he replied. "We're going to talk."

"I like the way you say that."

"What?"

"Aye."

"Why?"

"It seems to mean more than just 'yes'. It seems to mean, I don't know, 'we're on the same page', something like that."

"Are we on the same page, Alex? Because I, for one, feel like I'm stumbling around in a three volume edition of 'War and Peace'."

"What exactly do you want to be on the same page about?"

"Everything."

"Everything," she echoed, tilting her head a little, still a study in disingenuous innocence. "Well I have a few things I need to talk to you about. Maybe that would be a start."

"What are they?"

"My position here for one. All of a sudden I seem to be your only PA—for the time being."

"That's right. Caroline needed one and Vera was the obvious choice."

"Why Vera and not me? Is it as Vera says, because she's 'high-level'?"

JP placed his hand over his mouth and regarded Alex with open suspicion. "Are you saying you want to work for Caroline?"

Alex pondered the question. "No," she admitted finally, "I'd just like to know how the decision came about when the last conversation we had about this you said you didn't want me to be your PA."

"I didn't say that. I said I wanted you to be my paralegal."

"You still haven't answered my question."

"The partners thought you should go to Caroline. I intervened and suggested Vera instead on the basis that she's had more experience here and will be better placed to help Caroline settle in." JP paused as he took in Alex's slightly dissatisfied look before explaining. "Vera and I are like oil and water Alex, you know that. You on the other hand can read my mind and I like telepathy in a PA," he added with a deliberately challenging smile as he waited for her reaction.

"Is that right? What else do you like in a PA?" she tossed at him, narrowing her eyes in challenging rejoinder.

But JP knew he was a long way off telepathy himself at that moment. In fact, he was having more trouble reading her than he ever had before.

Essentially she was still the same old Alex but there was something different about her. She was more lighthearted and flirtatious, yet more cryptic and aloof too. But one thing was for sure. She was nothing if not the sexiest woman he had ever known and he wanted her so badly at that moment it actually hurt.

Unfortunately wanting her was one thing. Having her, another.

For weeks he'd been pressuring her to stand up for herself and make her own decisions. Now she'd done just that. But did he have any future in the life of this new Alex who was reinventing herself before his eyes? He had no reason to think so. Two nights ago she'd effectively shown him the door and now she was barely less than cool towards him.

"In a PA I'll settle for brains, spirit, loyalty, and the best set of legs in running shorts I've ever seen," he answered her with a short laugh.

"You know I could sue you for that comment."

"I don't care. By the way, Michael Porter wants to ask you out. I overheard him asking someone whether you're single or not, on the way back from the game this morning. Are you single, Alex?"

"You know I am," she replied quietly, the merest of quavers in her voice as she hit that sensitive topic.

"I didn't think you'd be able to stand up to all the family expectation, all the history."

"It wasn't easy." She looked agitated suddenly as though she didn't trust herself to discuss the topic without breaking down. "But about work..."

"Of course!" JP ran his hand through his hair as his chest heaved with a sigh. Yet again she was pushing him back to an arms length position. "Work. What do you want to know?"

"Lots of things have changed for me..." she began, turning away from him and taking some steps towards the windows.

He followed and stood behind her. "Do you want me to request a transfer for you, away from me? Is that what you're building up to this afternoon?"

He was bringing the conversation to a speedy climax but he couldn't bear the suspense of not knowing how she felt about him. He was banking on the fact that if she gave him some hint of what she wanted from him at work it might give him a hint about what she wanted from him in the rest of her life. There was one line he would not cross though: he would not pressure her into a relationship with him. If the two of them had a future it would be Alex's decision and Alex's decision only.

She swung around to him. "I don't want to be transferred."

Relief flooded through JP, intoxicating and sweet, but he counselled himself against haste.

"What *do* you want then?"

"I want to work with you as a paralegal and study law. So I'd very much like to take up the firm's offer if it's still open, thank you."

"Of course it's open. But as for working with me, I'm afraid I don't know what my future holds."

"I know that."

"You'll probably be left high and dry. You may not get any notice before I head back to the UK. Now that Caroline is here there's every possibility that will happen. It's not in your interests to wait and see and you should talk to HR about a transfer. I could get a temp for now."

"I'll take my chances," she declared decidedly. "And don't worry, I'll be completely professional, despite what's happened between us."

"I'm not the slightest bit concerned about what's happened between us." He dismissed her words instantly, wondering whether she was quite as emotionally detached from him as he'd thought. He decided another question might test her mettle a little. "What do you think of Caroline, by the way?"

Alex blew out through pursed lips and looked away from him to collect her thoughts for a few seconds before looking back again.

"She's incredible," she answered with resigned honesty. "She's beautiful, clever, charming. And just to top it off Sophie tells me she has some aristocratic pedigree going back to the Tudors and flies her own plane. She's so overawing I feel as if I should curtsy in front of her."

JP covered his mouth with his hand to conceal a smile. He didn't want Alex to think he was mocking her when as far as he was concerned Caroline simply wasn't in her league.

"Don't underestimate yourself, Alex. Anyway, forget Caroline. I want to run through where we are now. For a start, you and I are going to maintain a strictly professional relationship at all times," he began, breathing in the scent of lavender from her hair. "And you're going to stick with me until any day now I simply won't turn up in my office because I'm on a plane back to London. At that point you'll resolve to press on with the rest of your life—without me."

Alex nodded and his heart moved north into his throat. How could he feel like he did about her and she feel nothing? It just couldn't be possible, could it?

"It's a bit clinical but I think that's pretty much it," she replied eventually but her voice was hoarse.

"It's completely clinical! And that's all you want?"

Alex was staring up at him now. He couldn't help roaming her face like searchlights in the dark, willing her to take a leap of faith and utter the words he ached to hear.

And of course Alex did want more. She knew that having him in her life as just her boss would never, ever be enough. She would be tortured every single minute by his untouchable presence. For JP was the manifestation of a promise she'd carried around in her heart forever. The emptiness he would create if he carried on with his life without her would be unfathomable.

"Al, please," he murmured, his voice heavy with need. "Tell me now if that's all you want from me."

In that instant there was a short, sharp knock at the door and without hesitation Caroline Cartwright emerged from behind it.

"Oh, there you are," she announced in her silky, slightly bored voice. "I've been looking for you everywhere, JP." Her clear grey eyes surveyed the scene with cool distance. But Blind Freddy could have guessed Alex and JP were not discussing the latest dictation system or the delays in the office mailroom deliveries.

"I was right here all the time."

"There's a partners' meeting on now," she advised, looking Alex up and down with disdain as though noticing her for the first time.

Unable to bear the blood pounding in her ears as the tension rose between the three of them, Alex moved out from her position between JP and the window. Straightening herself she looked at him and asked in a strong, steady voice, "Would you like me to respond to Mark Jackson for you?"

He shook his head. "No, leave him to me. I'll ring him when I get back."

Alex nodded and walked towards the door, not bothering to make eye contact with Caroline.

"Oh, Alex," Caroline purred suddenly as Alex moved around her to leave JP's office.

She looked across at Caroline, startled at being addressed by her.

"Yes, Caroline," she heard herself reply in a clear, collected voice, surprising herself with her own composure.

"I've got some mail to go out and Vera's terribly busy. Be a pet and take it down to the mailroom for me, will you?"

Alex didn't reply. She could only gape at Caroline who was holding her gaze with a fixed, unflinching expression.

Alex had no problem helping other lawyers in the office and did it regularly. But Caroline's request was different. It was a demonstration of authority from management to an employee, for demonstration's sake. And Alex had no doubt it was done in response to the intimate scene she'd just walked in on.

Alex stood fixed to her spot, overwhelmed by the notion that she was immersed in one of those watershed moments in life where dignity was up for grabs. Caroline continued to hold her gaze with unwavering serenity.

Steeling her spine Alex opened her mouth to refuse in a manner that was so offensively rude it would undoubtedly bring about the immediate end of her employment at Griffen Murphy. But before she could utter a syllable JP's strident response had reached her ears, "Alex has more important things to do than run your errands, Caroline. Find someone else."

Alex swung around to take JP in as he stood where she'd left him, his arms crossed, his head tilted to one side in irritation, his mouth set in stony determination. And in a daze of tumultuous emotions she walked out of his office.

Chapter Thirteen

It was turning out to be the longest week of her life. Alex thought it would never end. She tried to bury herself in work and keep her thoughts occupied but it was useless. JP filled her mind and her heart and there was simply no way of shaking him loose.

Shortly after the run-in with Caroline in his office he'd disappeared into a meeting with his partners and didn't reappear for the rest of that day, or Friday either for that matter. Early the following Monday morning he left for Queensland to deal with Mark Jackson's injunction application and didn't return until Wednesday night.

As for Thursday and Friday, they may as well have been ships in the night. He was either in court or in protracted meetings with clients or his partners. If he did reappear the lawyers would swoop to pick his brains about their own matters. He'd then slice his time up into as many portions as he could as they either queued at his door or pressured Alex to squeeze them into his diary. Even Caroline was reduced to making an appointment to see him.

Alex thanked her lucky stars for the distraction of the work he was piling upon her every day from his remote locations. Every morning she'd find a string of messages or emails from his phone. As he didn't have time for dictation he'd give her the bare bones of what he needed and then leave the drafting to her. By the next morning it had rematerialised as a pile on her desk, marked-up or signed off and accompanied by a long string of instructions for that day.

If and how he was getting any sleep Alex just couldn't imagine. The workload suggested he was up most of the night trying to make up for the hours during the day when he was pulled in three different directions at once. Whenever she had a fleeting glimpse of him she could tell he was exhausted.

Alex wished there were something more she could do to help but he kept a professional distance from her. The promise she'd made to do the same was fresh in her mind too. How could she reverse that now when they'd effectively evicted each other from their lives just ten days ago? How did such a fragile, tentative beginning as they'd shared ever recover from that?

At half past five on the Friday, having seen JP for a grand total of five minutes that day, Alex tidied up her desk and swinging her handbag onto her shoulder wandered over to Sophie.

"Hello you," Sophie greeted her brightly. "Coming to Friday night drinks?"

"No thanks, I'm not in the mood. I thought I'd go to the gym instead. But if you feel like it, would you like to meet up later and see a movie?"

In truth, Alex was dreading the thought of trying to fill up yet another weekend with her own company as she battled the endless distraction of JP: where he was, what he was doing, who he was with.

"Sure, but there's one condition. I want you to buck up. You've had the personality of a wet blanket lately and I'm sick of it. No excuses."

Alex laughed at Sophie's grim summation of her personality. "Has it been that bad?"

Sophie stuck out her bottom lip and shot up her eyebrows in mockery of Alex's demeanour.

"You know how they say dogs resemble their owners? Well you're beginning to resemble your boss when he's having one of his 'I want it done yesterday' fits."

Alex laughed again. "I get the picture."

"Good, then belt up. I know you've had the fortnight from hell with all the Simon drama topped off with the most demanding yet invisible boss in the world but it could be worse," Sophie finished before raising her hand to cover her mouth and hiss at her in a whisper, "You could be working for Caroline Cartwright!"

Alex changed into her gym gear in the ladies and was about to step into the lift when Michael Porter appeared in front of her from out of the stairwell.

"Alex Farrer!" he announced as a smile lit up his face. "Just the person I'm looking for. I hear you're about to start as a paralegal."

"It hasn't been finalised yet. I've been pretty flat out with Jonathan's PA work anyway."

"I know, but I was hoping you might be able to give me a hand with something if I can clear it with the boss next week. It's a whopping file—five parts. It needs a full brief and observations and I'm completely swamped. It would be great to have some help with it."

"I'm sure that would be okay," she thought out loud. "I could probably stay back next week and work on it. Or I could get in early—that way it won't interfere with my other work."

"That would be great."

"In fact," Alex began again brightly, "I've got a clear weekend. Why don't you give me the first two or three parts from the file now and I'll take them home."

"Are you sure? I don't want to wreck your weekend."

"No, you won't," she reassured him, relieved she would have something to keep her busy for two whole days. "I was planning on spending some time at home anyway. I can read the file and then get Jonathan's okay on Monday."

But Michael was watching her with an odd expression.

"What is it?"

"You do know, don't you Alex?"

"Know what?

"Jonathan McKenzie's gone."

"Gone where?" Alex heard herself croak weakly.

"Back to London. He left the office this morning to go home and pack up his place. His flight leaves tonight."

"When is he coming back?" Alex asked but sensed Michael's answer would be the worst possible answer she could have.

"He's not. Caroline's taking over litigation. Didn't he tell you? You're his PA! I can't believe he didn't tell you! My God, are you okay? You're as pale as!"

"I'm fine," she assured him but nothing could have been further from the truth. The office around her was spinning and she felt sick to her stomach.

Everything she'd believed about JP was splintering around her. He'd left her without a word, just as he said he would. She was so irrelevant at every level of his life he hadn't even found it necessary to let her know he was going.

"Okay." Michael was still looking doubtfully at Alex. "If you're sure you're all right then I'll go upstairs and get the file now. I'm due at a client's drinks at half past six so am heading out myself. I'll be back in five minutes."

With that Michael vanished into the stairwell again to return to his office whilst Alex stood stock-still, saying goodbye in a dazed fashion to various colleagues as they strolled past and got into lifts.

At first the shock of Michael's news overwhelmed her but within a few short minutes it had begun to subside and anger became a voracious animal tearing her apart. Even putting aside the closeness that had crept up between them, how could he dump his PA like that, leaving her with no boss and an uncertain future?

But at that moment her mobile phone rang.

"Yes!" Alex barked down the line in a rage, certain it would be JP and determined to tell him exactly what she thought of him.

"Alex, it's me," Sophie began tentatively in response to Alex's explosion.

"Sorry Soph, I thought you were someone else."

"Then I feel sorry for them, whoever they are. Perhaps I shouldn't keep you too long if you're expecting a call but I need to tell you something about Jonathan McKenzie."

"If you're going to tell me he's gone then I already know."

"Ah, I see." Sophie murmured with an understanding voice. "Are you okay?"

"Not really. I'm furious. How did you know he'd gone?"

"Oh, um, Justin Murphy just told me. Apparently the decision was only made today. I gather the London office is in trouble without a managing partner there. Some huge piece of litigation is about to come through the door so he's getting on an eight o'clock Qantas flight tonight. Oh, by the way, do you mind if I take a rain check on the movies tonight? I'm a bit done in."

"That's fine Soph, of course. Thanks for letting me know about Jonathan too."

Alex rang off and beside her the lift doors opened. Strangely though, there was nobody inside and no one had called it to her floor. Alex gazed into its empty space, overcome with the notion that the inanimate object next to her was calling her to action.

Without a second's further thought Alex entered the lift and pressed the ground floor button. Michael Porter and his file would have to wait.

Chapter Fourteen

Playing Russian roulette with life was not for the faint hearted. Alex was discovering that very quickly. But as she sat in the backseat of the cab on her way to the airport she revelled in the fact that at least now she was the one tossing the gambling chips into the game of life—it was nothing short of exhilarating.

But her odds in the game she was in couldn't be good. Even putting aside the unpredictable reception she might receive from JP, whether she would find him out at the airport was less than certain. International departures were chaotic at the best of times and he could have checked in by now and be waiting in some flight lounge she couldn't get into.

Her other problem was time. From memory, check-in for international flights was ninety minutes before departure. If he was going at eight then he'd have to check-in by six-thirty. It had just gone six o'clock so she would be running very close to missing him completely.

To make matters worse it seemed every red light was plotting against her. She squirmed and wriggled impatiently, willing each one to return to green immediately. Over and over again she silently cursed the poor driver for his adherence to the road rules and his careful driving. Yet eventually he swung up into the departures drop off zone and handing him notes to more than cover the fare she jumped out of the cab without waiting for change and ran into the terminal.

Searching the airport crowds like a strobe light she did some quick circuits around the long, snakelike queues of people winding backwards and forwards in front of the check-in desks, their luggage piled high in front of them. But there was no JP.

Scanning the screens listing departures she found a Qantas flight bound for London that was due to leave at eight. That had to be the one he was going on and yet she'd circled the whole Qantas check-in area several times and there was still no sign of him.

With a galloping pulse and a nervous gait to her walk she paced anxiously through the crowd, searching hopelessly for that mop of dark blonde hair, the chiseled jawline and cheekbones, the penetrating blue eyes. Yet with every passing minute hope was dying inside her. He simply wasn't there, and no amount of roaming through the crowd would change that.

As anger dissolved into despair she finally sunk down onto a chair and dropped her head into her hands. JP had clearly gone through immigration and would not be coming out. Very soon he'd be on a plane heading back to the UK leaving more questions than answers plaguing their short relationship. And with searing pain ripping her apart she wondered whether she'd ever see him again.

"Do you mind if we sit down?"

Alex sat up and removed her hands from her face to see a young mother with two small children standing in front of her.

"No, no, of course. Please do," Alex replied quickly as she shifted herself up to one end of the bench. The woman gave her an appreciative smile and Alex returned it before gazing out across the crowd again. And that was when she saw him.

JP McKenzie was strolling around the check-in area, not more than ten metres away from her. He was without luggage and his hands were resting casually in his pockets as though he might be looking for someone. Alex climbed slowly to her feet but then she couldn't move any further. She didn't have to.

As though sensing the weight of her gaze at his back he swung around and spotted her immediately.

Alex watched him in disbelief, doubting her own eyes. But then she knew she could never have conjured up the expression on his face as he regarded her thoughtfully; he was giving nothing away.

Alex folded her arms. Now that she'd found him she felt grumpy again. But then a smirk crossed JP's mouth and he crossed his own arms, mimicking her own feisty stance, tilting his head to one side in challenge.

She walked towards him and he eyed her curiously, his gaze drifting over her figure in her gym gear. She stopped about a metre in front of him, her arms still crossed, her lips pressed together in taut repression of the anxiety and ecstasy of seeing him again.

"What can I do for you?" he asked smoothly.

"Can't you guess?" Alex snapped, revealing more nervousness than she wanted to.

"Enlighten me," he crooned, his dark blue-eyed look resting heavily upon her.

"An explanation would be nice," she blurted. "About how you feel comfortable leaving like this without letting me know you're going."

JP regarded her with a mixture of amusement and seriousness. "It was all very sudden."

"That doesn't explain why you didn't tell me you were leaving. You have my phone numbers."

JP regarded her with a cool stare and shrugged. "Do you think it was absolutely necessary? You've only been working for me for a month, after all."

Alex smarted at the rejection and looked away into the crowd to collect herself before going on.

It was not turning out well.

She was already picturing herself climbing into a cab to go home alone that night. Yet she was determined to speak from the heart once and for all before he vanished out of her life for good.

"You know it's been more than just a one month job for me."

"Has it, Alex?" he threw at her immediately. "You've spent most of that month telling me you don't want me in your life. What is it that you do want from me exactly? Why are you here?"

Alex stared wildly at him. He didn't have feelings for her after all. She was about to make a big fat fool of herself. In fact, she already had by appearing at the airport in the first place. But then without another thought she jumped into the emotional abyss of blue and bottomless icy depths lying in wait for her.

"I needed to see you one more time," she began unsteadily but soon summoned her courage and locked her eyes with his, her voice following in its calm wake. "I know I shouldn't be here. You're right. I only worked for you for a month and that's not a foundation for anything is it? Yet despite that, I'm so sad you're leaving JP. I'll miss you. I'm already missing you. The last month has been the worst and yet because of you, the most wonderful of my life. Anyway, that's all I wanted to say."

Alex swung around and began to walk towards the exit doors, hurriedly wiping away the tears rolling down her cheeks. She'd said what she came to say but couldn't bear to linger for the rejection he was about to dish out.

But in the next moment JP had caught her arm and was swinging her around. His two hands were holding her so firmly she couldn't have moved if she'd tried.

"If you could choose anything," he began, his voice husky and urgent, his eyes burning into hers before he repeated himself, "If you could choose anything right now, what would it be?"

Alex stared at him but the truth filled her heart and overflowed before she replied, "To be with you."

"Why, Alex?"

"Because I love you..."

JP gave her a half-wild look as he took her head in his hands and devoured her with his eyes.

"Then come with me."

Alex was giddy. It was too much. It wasn't happening. It sounded as if it wasn't over, but she had to be dreaming. Any minute now she'd wake up from the dream and discover that JP was long gone from the country and from her life.

"What?" she whispered. "How can I?"

"This is how," JP smiled at her, dropping his hands from her head to draw paperwork from his inside pocket and hand it to her. In a blur she could see references to E-tickets, Qantas and Alex Farrer.

She looked up at JP in startled confusion. "You want me to come with you to England?"

JP nodded and cupped her face with his hand. "More than anything in the world. Of course if you don't want to then we'll stay here. Somehow I'll work out another arrangement for the London office."

"No, I want to go," Alex gushed helplessly. "More than you can imagine. It's important for the firm that you're there and it'll be an adventure for me, and going there with you is … well, it's like a dream coming true. But are you talking about a permanent move?"

"Maybe, but it's up to you Al. You'll need time to think about where you want to live and what you'd like to do in terms of work and study. Let's go for a month or two and see how we like it."

"Okay then," Alex laughed, her head swimming with the exhilarating uncertainties swarming into her life. "So I'm going to get on a plane tonight, in gym clothes?"

"Do you get the feeling this relationship of ours is coming round to full circle? Here we are standing in a public place again and discussing your clothing options."

And then Alex felt it: the cold hard slap of reality showstopper. "Oh God, JP," she whispered portentously. "What about Mum and Dad? I can't disappear on them like this. They're elderly and I'm the only one they've got."

With another foray into the inside of his suit jacket JP produced a passport and handed it to her.

"Who do you think gave me this?" he explained gently. "I went to see them last week, after you'd refused a transfer away from me. I was sure that if you didn't care for me you would have jumped at a move. But I also knew you wouldn't want to leave your parents without their blessing, even for a short time. But they support this Alex. They both agreed it would be a great opportunity for you to live your own life for a while. Ring them if you like, they'll tell you that themselves."

Alex studied the passport in a daze. It was hers. Of course it was hers. But she was having trouble believing anything at that moment.

"I can't believe Mum and Dad are happy about me taking off like this," she murmured.

"I think the clincher may have been when I told them I'd loved you from the first day we met and I couldn't stand to leave the country without you."

Alex smiled at JP. "You said that?"

He grinned back. "I did, Alex," he whispered and taking her face again in his hands he leaned in to kiss her tenderly and slowly, driving her pulse wild and prompting her to burrow her hands inside his jacket, laying them against his warm chest. Was it really possible that she could snuggle up against him anytime she wanted from now on?

But then she broke away, the awful possibilities of that night surging through her. "But you left our entire future in my hands. What if I hadn't come tonight? What if I hadn't known you were going?"

"I took out an insurance policy," he smirked wryly. "I phoned Sophie."

Alex shook her head. "I don't understand."

"I told her I had a job for her. She was to phone you and let you know I was flying home tonight. It was risky. I couldn't be sure you'd turn up but I had to take that chance. Our flight's not until 9.30 by the way, in case you're thinking I was cutting things a bit fine."

"And Sophie agreed to do that? No questions asked?"

JP nodded.

"I can't believe it. It's not like Sophie to be such a dark horse. She didn't let on at all, although she got off the phone in a big hurry."

"Well that would be because I told her to ring me back as soon as she'd reached you. You'll have to put her out of her misery soon. I could tell she was desperate to know what was going on."

Alex gave JP a serious look. "What is going on JP? Why didn't you tell me you were leaving?"

He raised a hand to push a strand of dark hair away from her cheek. "I needed to know that choosing me was entirely your decision. Your parents and Simon have been steering your life for a long time and you've let them do that. I have no intention of taking over that role."

"I would never feel..." Alex interjected but JP lay a finger on her lips to silence her.

"You said it yourself, the night I drove you home from your parents. Remember? You said I was laying down the blueprints for your life, just like your father and Simon."

"I didn't mean you."

"You did and you were right to say it. I can be pushy. All those years protecting my mother had a big impact on the way I run my life. Sometimes it spills over to the people closest to me—just ask Adam and Justin; they often tell me to pull my head in when I start to take over. You'll have to keep me to heel on that too."

"I will," Alex breathed, a rush of happiness coursing through her as she listened to him talk so easily of their future.

"I meant what I said about that first morning we met," he murmured seriously. "I watched you for a while before I approached you on that street; you were so serene and so still in all that weather and chaos. I was glad you were going to be my PA because I desperately wanted some of that serenity in my working life, but I had no idea how much I would come to want it in every part of my life."

"All I know about that first day is how relieved I was when I left the boutique thinking I'd never see you again," Alex admitted. "The way you made me feel ... it frightened the hell out of me. I'd never felt anything like that with Simon. I hadn't even known it was possible to feel that way."

"I'm sorry you had to go through that with Simon, for all our sakes," he murmured. "I wish we could have had a different beginning, and I did try and keep my distance from you. But meeting Simon that night at your parents' house changed everything for me. I couldn't sit back and watch you throw your life away on a loveless marriage, even though I was far from confident you'd want anything to do with me when it was all over."

"It was a nightmare, wasn't it?" Alex nodded. "I was so ashamed of my feelings for you. That's why I fought them so hard. But it was that morning with Simon at Bellevue Hill and then that night with you which changed everything for me. I knew then that I was deceiving Simon. There was a huge part of myself I'd kept hidden from him from years because I knew he wouldn't like it. The problem was he'd ended up engaged to a girl he barely knew."

JP nodded. "So which girl have I got here?" he replied with a grin.

"The one you noticed straight away. The one I'd hidden away from the world for far too long."

"You mean the bright, beautiful and determined Alex Farrer."

"I think you've forgotten some of the less attractive traits," Alex laughed, but felt herself flush with his compliment.

"Oh those!" JP declared with a guffaw. "You mean the mulishness, the quick temper and the 'stick your head in the sand like an ostrich' tendencies."

"That's probably a fairer balance, especially as I'll have to live with your special ways."

"Okay, spit them out," he smiled challengingly.

"Let's see. We have the 'my way or the highway' approach to life, the impatience, the changeability. Vera couldn't stand working for you, you know. She told me so," Alex teased.

"Aye right. So how did you stand it?"

"Because when I'm with you I'm true to myself," Alex began seriously. "And because everything you say makes complete sense to me. And because you're kind and smart and decent ... oh, and a great kisser too, of course."

JP watched her for a few moments and then pressing his lips together he gathered her up in his arms and cuddled her very close. But as if on cue an announcement called all passengers on their flight to the check-in counter.

"We should go," Alex murmured and JP released her reluctantly, taking her hand in his.

After going through immigration, he headed off to the bookshop so that Alex could shop for an outfit to wear on the plane. She bought a long sleeved black fitted dress made of comfortable stretchy fabric and a pair of long black boots. She was glad to stow her gym gear in a bag. But despite immersing herself in practicalities she was still having trouble believing the incredible turn her life had taken.

And JP was having the same trouble as he watched Alex wander back towards the bookshop to meet him. She was swinging her bag by her side and walking tall. Then she was running a relaxed hand through her long dark hair so that it fell away from her face, casting her eyes curiously over the shop window displays on her left.

She clearly had no idea she was catching the eye of every single person she passed simply because she walked with such elegant grace. Yet before him was the girl who just weeks ago had been hiding herself from the world under more than just layers of mud, oil and nondescript clothing. In fact, she'd been so well hidden that the girl herself had almost forgotten she existed.

Alex noticed him waiting for her and smiled. Then she was in his arms and they were holding on to each other as though they hadn't seen each other in weeks before she pulled away and stroked the renegade lock of hair away from his forehead.

"I love you, JP McKenzie," she said tenderly.

He sighed a deep, satisfied sigh, and said, "Aye, Alex Farrer. I love you too."

ALSO AVAILABLE FROM ESCAPE PUBLISHING...

His Brand of Beautiful
by Lily Malone

When marketing strategist Tate Newell first meets wine executive Christina Clay, he has one goal in mind: tell Christina he won't design the new brand for Clay Wines. Tell her thanks, but no thanks. So long, good night.

But Tate is a sucker for a damsel in distress and when a diary mix-up leaves Christina in his debt, Tate gets more than he bargained for.

What does a resourceful girl do when the best marketing brain in the business won't play ball? She bluffs. She cheats. And she ups the ante. But when the stakes get too high, does anybody win?

Falling in love was never part of this branding brief.

Makeover Miracle
by Charmaine Ross

Abbey Miller and her friend Jennifer have been picked from a live audience to take part in reality television show Makeover Miracle. This is Abbey's worst nightmare, and brings back deep memories of being teased and the brunt of cruel jokes. The last thing

Abbey wants is her soul to be laid bare for the whole of Australia to see, but being the true friend she is, she agrees to help Jennifer, who desperately wants to change her life.

Quinn Campbell, the producer of Makeover Miracle can see Abbey crumbling live on stage, and after she vomits into a wastepaper basket, goes to her aid, not expecting see such a sad, haunted look in her eyes. There's something about Abbey that reaches out to him. The look in her eyes brings back long buried memories of his sister and his failure as a brother to help her.

This is a story about one woman's journey through harsh emotional abuses and the man who is able to make her believe in herself. Set against the beautiful Dandenong Ranges, *Makeover Miracle* is a story about forgiveness, understanding, personal growth and, of course, falling in love with that one special person.

Under the Hood
by Juanita Kees

When Scott Devin buys a struggling car dealership in semi-rural Western Australia, the last person he expects to see in charge is a stilletto-wearing, mini-skirted foreperson. Exactly the distraction a struggling, male-dominated workshop doesn't need! But there's more to TJ Stevens than meets the eye.

TJ Stevens has two major goals in life: to preserve her grandfather's heritage and protect her teenage rehabilitation program—and she'll go to any lengths to do it. Scott Devin's presence is a threat to everything she's worked hard to achieve, so keeping him at arms length shouldn't be a problem ... or will it?

Printed in Great Britain
by Amazon